MARIGOLD MIND LAUNDRY

MARIGOLD MIND LAUNDRY

THE SOUL-STIRRING KOREAN BESTSELLER

JUNGEUN YUN

Translated by Shanna Tan

THE DIAL PRESS
NEW YORK

Published in the United States by The Dial Press,
an imprint of Random House,
a division of Penguin Random House LLC, New York.

The Dial Press is a registered trademark and the
colophon is a trademark of Penguin Random House LLC.

Originally published in Korean by Book Romance in 2023. This
translation published in the United Kingdom by Doubleday,
an imprint of Transworld. Transworld is part of the
Penguin Random House Group of companies.

Hardback ISBN 9780593733936
Ebook ISBN 9780593733943

Printed in the United States of America on acid-free paper

randomhousebooks.com

2 4 6 8 9 7 5 3 1

First U.S. Edition

What if . . .

What if it's possible to wash away your regrets,
the pain crusted into stubborn stains?
If only you could scrub away the hurt,
would that make you feel better?

If that most painful memory could be forever gone,
would you finally be happy?

THE DREAM

Somewhere on Earth was a village where spring faded into autumn, and after autumn, spring returned once more. Spin the globe round and round and you'd eventually see it, the size of a speck of dust. Yet nobody knew of its existence. The village was home to mysterious plants and trees, and people who held powers beyond imagination. Beautiful people you'd easily mistake for fairies, only they didn't have wings.

Life in the village was like a bed of flowers. Dazzling blue sky, the weather never too hot or cold. The harvest was bountiful, and the laughter, endless. The villagers all had kind eyes and a warm heart. Hate, pain, sadness – such feelings didn't exist. Never would you hear a sharp word exchanged. It was always peaceful.

Possessing wondrous powers, the villagers were a beacon of light, bringing warmth wherever they went. When the moon rose, they danced under its silvery orb, and when the sun shone, their smiles were warm and bright. They'd never known the cold. Not the biting wind that whipped the face, nor the callousness in hearts that hunched shoulders.

But one day, the fiery passion of summer arrived unannounced, setting one man's heart ablaze.

'Hello, can you hear me? Are you OK?'

'I . . .'

'What did you say? I can't hear you.'

'Water . . .'

'Water? Of course! Here you go.'

The man had been walking along a narrow path that wound through the village. As the village custodian, he was responsible for all matters, big or small. He swung his arms, breathing in the scents of the greenery, when he spotted a figure lying unconscious on the path. A woman with long, dark hair, and the fairest of skin. When he gave her water, her lips quivered as if to speak. After taking a few tiny sips, she passed out again. *She's not from our village*, he thought.

'Hey, wake up! Where do you live? I'll take you home.'

He hovered over her, but there was no response. Conscious that her white dress might get dirty, he shrugged off his jacket and draped it over her before sitting down.

This is no place to be sleeping . . . Well, I guess she doesn't have much choice. I'll take her home when she wakes up. Oh wait . . . I feel a bit sleepy . . . How strange . . .

The man rested his head comfortably on his knees and drifted off to sleep.

'Excuse me, hello? Where are we?'

Feeling a gentle nudge on his shoulder, the man stirred awake and found himself drawn into a pair of blue eyes, deep and mysterious, as if he were staring into the ocean or the sky. In the light, they were a brilliant shade of cobalt. But when she blinked, the orbs behind her long lashes took on a russet hue. For a moment, he lost himself.

'We're . . . er, I . . . This is the village of wondrous powers.'

'Wondrous powers?' the woman echoed. 'It smells so different here. I can read a place's energy by its scent, you know . . . And it smells good here. Peaceful, yet somewhat nostalgic, too. How strange. Even the wind here feels gentler. If only I could live here, too.'

'Well . . . would you like to stay here with me?'

The man scrambled to his feet, shocked by his own boldness. She fixed her gaze on him as he shuffled awkwardly, his ears blushing. A radiant smile lit up her face.

'I would.'

Calling it love at first sight was rather a cliché, but the woman settled down in the village and soon bore a beautiful daughter. The villagers might hold mysterious powers, but never once did they use them for anything but good. Through the seasons of falling leaves and new beginnings, the family of three lived happily.

Life was perfectly blissful, yet one day the woman became seized by an inexplicable feeling of anxiety.

No, no, nothing's going to happen. I'm probably the only one here who even knows what anxiety is . . .

She shook her head, trying to rid herself of the unease.

As night fell, the lights across the village flickered out, leaving the house to bask in a comforting glow. Over the years, the husband and wife had grown more alike, the same gentle expression shaping their kind features. In the dim light of the bedside lamp, they often lay in bed holding hands, chatting until their eyelids grew heavy with sleep.

In the time it took for age to streak their hair grey, their sweet daughter blossomed into a young woman. But today, her mother looked over at her husband. She felt unusually troubled.

'Darling, don't you think we should tell her about her powers?'

'Hmm, it's still too soon.'

'What do you mean, too soon? She's coming of age next year. She needs to know how to control her abilities and to use them only when necessary.'

'But she has no idea about them at all. It'll come as a huge shock.'

'That's true.'

'We will find a good time soon.'

'OK. And once she knows, we must keep her away from reading about the outside world, at least for the time being.'

'We'd better. Those books contain too many unfamiliar emotions that may affect her powers.'

Some signs had begun to show recently, and the woman fretted. She had been convinced her daughter had inherited her own lack of powers. On the rare occasion that the woman had sensed this might not be the case, she'd waved it aside, attributing her daughter's behaviour to a strong sense of empathy, and her ability to focus on her goals. But, for the chosen ones, those who did possess this power, there was no escape from the trials and tribulations life held for them.

To fail to master their powers would mean they would never fully blossom, and they would be destined to wander in search of a way to heal the bruises in their heart. Those who triumphed would see their powers unfurl to shine a light in the world.

These people could expect a good life, but it would also be tinged with loneliness and melancholy. Like the two faces of the moon, the brighter the light, the darker the shadows.

The girl's mother had stumbled upon the village after fleeing from her city. And love had healed her, made her whole again. Now she yearned for her child to be like a flower that would never wilt, someone who would never know pain, who would live a carefree life in this most beautiful village tucked away from the world.

It was a matter of time before she was reminded that wishes were often wishful thinking. It soon dawned on the couple that their daughter soothed their hearts, and that she had an uncanny ability to make her own wishes come true. In no time, she would have to go through a range of unfamiliar emotions and prepare to leave home. In their village, only the chosen ones would venture into the outside world to do good with their powers. Signs that they had such powers for good were usually detected early, and so the younger children could be sent to training school. But the woman's daughter turned out to be a special case, her powers emerging later, when she was coming of age.

'I-I have . . . powers?'

The girl froze and her heart pounded. After reading late into the night, she'd come out to get a cup of water but ended up following the light seeping out from the crack under the door to her parents' bedroom. *What kind of powers? Who should I be helping? Do I have to leave the village like the other chosen ones? What surprises will the outside world hold?* She was flooded with both unease and expectation. She leaned against the wall and listened to her parents from behind the door.

'Has anyone from the village ever had two powers?'

'I heard there was someone, a century ago.'

The answer was met with silence.

Outside the door, the girl's knees buckled. She grabbed the wall to steady herself before stumbling into a chair. That she was a chosen one was already a huge shock. But did she actually have double powers? It was as if someone had turned her world upside down. She stared out of the window. The sky felt deeper, darker. The moon and the stars were hiding behind an inky blanket.

A door to the outside world had opened.

I'll be fine. Nothing's going to happen . . .

She closed her eyes and tried to steady her breathing. *One, two, three . . .*

'Mum! Dad! Don't go. Please, come back . . .'

The girl jerked awake, tears streaming down her face. She'd had a nightmare. In her dream, her family had disappeared into the tumultuous winds of a tornado. The storm had swept up everything she held dear, leaving her behind. A strange feeling welled up within her. Was this what she'd read about? The feeling called *anxiety*? Or was it *fear*? Her parents had forbidden her to read any stories about the outside world before bedtime, but curiosity had got the better of her. She often borrowed books from the restricted access shelf in the library and secretly read them under the covers while her parents were asleep. Just yesterday evening, she'd read a fascinating story of a character who crosses time and space in search of her family, who'd vanished into a magic black hole.

She placed a hand over her chest to comfort herself as she wept. Strange. Her parents would have heard her sobbing. Why weren't they rushing over to check on her? Why was everything so quiet? Were they still fast asleep? Was this all a dream? The air was unusually stale. Her sense of unease began to swell. She looked up, rubbed her eyes, blinked several times, gave them another good rub.

No matter what she did, she was still consumed by a feeling

of emptiness. *This must be a dream. An actual nightmare. Sleep.* She needed to sleep and then to fall into a new dream. She squeezed her eyes shut.

Wait. Hadn't she been listening in on her parents before she fell asleep? Fragments of their conversation were coming back to her. Was this . . . not a dream?

'It's lovely to have the power to empathize and heal, but to have the ability to make wishes come true? This second power sounds dangerous, and too powerful.'

'How did we take so long to realize? If only we'd known earlier . . . she could have gone to training school. Now she has to learn everything by herself. It'll be so overwhelming.'

'Don't blame yourself. There's no point regretting what has already happened. We'll just have to support her as much as we can.'

'I suppose so. Didn't they warn that if you don't know how to control your power from the start, everything you think or dream of might come true? Let's make sure she doesn't think about anything negative. How about having a cosy evening tomorrow and easing her into the truth?'

'Yes, let's do that. And let's hope both her powers will fully blossom . . .'

How could she have dozed off right at that moment? The girl stewed in regret. She should not have fallen asleep. No, coming out of her room to fetch water had been a terrible idea. Why had she even eavesdropped on her parents? Nor should she have attempted to read any books from the outside world. Or even set foot in the restricted access section. The regrets snowballed, crushing her.

Her eyes flew open again. This was no dream. The feeling of stark emptiness around her still lingered.

She knew now she was all alone. Everyone she loved had disappeared.

Because of her.

If only I could turn back time. Would I have chosen differently? Could I have?

Wouldn't it have been even better if I'd been given the power of foresight – to prevent misfortune before it happened? I could have put a stop to this.

No, I refuse to accept this, to let everything I cherished vanish in a split second. All I did was fall asleep, but I woke up to find my beautiful world plunged into an endless darkness.

I am in a dream.

I must be.

In a dream.

Chapter I

THE CYCLE OF NEVER-ENDING REBIRTHS

'This is not a dream. This is real.'

Sometimes – no, too often – the cruelty of the real world cut more deeply than a dream.

Despite all efforts to open and close her eyes, or to fall back to sleep and to wake up again, she remained painfully awake and alone. She had not understood how to control her powers. And now she had caused her entire family to disappear.

I can set things right, I know I can, she told herself as she pored over a pile of books from the training school.

Finally, she found something.

From the start, take care *not* to dream at night. Even the slightest lack of control over your gift will mean that in the moment before you fall asleep anything you wish for will come true, even if it is merely an inadvertent or passing thought. To prevent any misuse of power, and to avoid

a potentially dangerous situation, you must meditate before bedtime and practise positive thinking.

A wave of despair crashed over her. She tried closing her eyes and counting to a hundred. But no matter how desperately she tried to fall into a dream of her family returning, she always woke up alone.

Could Mum and Dad have fallen into another world, just like the one in the story? Even if I have to comb through the whole universe, I'll find them. I promise. Time will wait for me. Surely, when I am reborn for the millionth time, we will be reunited? I will make everything right again.

There's a saying that people driven to the edge often find super-strength within themselves. Fuelled by her misery, the girl unknowingly tapped into her newfound powers, sealing her fate to wander the world in a cycle of never-ending rebirths. The warnings of danger meant nothing to her. What could be worse than losing her loved ones? Nor did she heed the words of caution to use her powers only for good as she set off on her seemingly eternal search for her family. In the intersection of time and space, the girl with the rosy cheeks began to lose her beautiful smile. She did not care how long it took to find her parents. Life after life, she continued to wander lost through the world.

Where are they? Please . . . let me find them,
or else, let this all be a bad dream.

Going through the motions of living life over and over was not enough – her efforts to track down her parents were in vain. All she managed to do was to rob herself of the freedom to die once and for all. As much as she wanted to find her loved ones, she was increasingly desperate to stop this never-ending cycle of rebirth. She yearned to grow old and really die, like any ordinary person. In her aching loneliness, she became immune to life's joy. *It's OK. Once I find my parents, I'll be able to smile again.* Consumed by this thought, she lived each life using her ability for no one but herself.

As time passed, her eyes clouded over with melancholy, and as she ceased to be able to cry, her face became a blank canvas. Loneliness seeped into her bones, she developed a vacant stare, and as she gradually stopped eating or even sleeping, she started to shrivel to skin and bone.

To ensure her parents would recognize her, she dared not stray very far from the age she'd been when they were separated. In some lives, she was a twenty-something, in others, in her thirties. On a couple of occasions, she lived as a forty-year-old, but never, ever older. Deep down, though, she knew that her real fear stemmed from the gradual loss of her childhood memories, and she might be the one to walk on by without recognizing them. Weariness filled her heart. Meanwhile, time – cruelly – continued to speed by.

Is it the millionth time yet? If only today were a dream.

Why weren't her wishes coming true? When would she be able to use her powers freely? She had no idea, and nothing was more futile than agonizing over a question with no answers. She felt a pang of regret. Maybe it hadn't been a good idea to leave the books from the training school behind in the village.

It was day one of a new life all over again. She opened her eyes, shuffled out of bed and grabbed the kettle.

Water, boil! Come on, blub blub . . . It's not too much to ask.

She muttered to herself out of habit as she lifted the lid to fill the kettle. She could wake up at whatever age she wanted, and wherever she wanted, keep her looks and even her home and her belongings. So why weren't her other wishes coming true?

'Hmm, where's my cup? It should be here . . .'

She craned her neck and rummaged around on the top shelf, moving on to the bottom drawer before finally catching sight of the white cup on the ledge right at eye level. She stared at it. Had it been there all the time?

The kettle whistled shrilly.

'I. Miss. Them.'

Saying it aloud made her ache with longing. She was exhausted. She'd never known any fun or happiness. But even as she rid herself of the freedom to feel, other people were a comforting presence. They stayed by her side without pressuring her, even though she had nothing to offer in return. But each time, just as she felt herself getting attached to them, she'd flee to her next life. Their faces flashed through her mind – all those who'd shown friendship towards her even as she kept her distance. Over and over, she found herself wishing she could stop wandering like a lost sheep and settle down.

'But what right do I have to do so?'

Whenever she caught herself wishing to settle anywhere, she took it as a sign to move on.

It wasn't like she was sad all the time. There were things she enjoyed, such as listening to other people's stories. Her ability to empathize allowed her to share their pain, and once they'd calmed down, she'd serve them some tea and watch their smiles slowly return to their faces.

She enjoyed the subtle shift in the air when people relaxed in her presence. It wasn't hard for her to listen to frustrating stories. Having lived much longer than anyone else, she naturally came to know that in life there were more difficult moments than happy ones. The stories people shared with her flowed like music to her ears.

Instead of burying any negativity and leaving long-lasting marks on their hearts, it was much better that they open up to her, as she could silently clear the dark clouds over them. A part of her hoped that if she could soothe more hearts, someday, hers too would be filled.

She knew this was her power. But what if she lost someone again? Did love always have to be accompanied by the fear of loss? Having frozen time for herself, whenever she saw people around her growing visibly older, she felt compelled to leave even when it was hard to walk away.

Sometimes she wondered if any of those people could be her lost loved ones. Was it possible she remained so mired in guilt from her mistake that she failed to realize what she was looking for had been right in front of her all along? Just like the white cup.

She reached out for it and poured in the water, deep in thought. Whether it was to boil the water or fill the cup, these were ultimately her choices. *OK, stop it*, she told herself firmly. Her thoughts were going nowhere. She'd reached a point where even going through the motions of rebirth was taking a huge toll on her. Should she try and give up? *No. Stop thinking like this*, she chided herself, shaking her head to erase her thoughts.

She blew at the steam rising over the cup, took careful sips and looked around her home. Despite waking up in a different neighbourhood each time, the layout of her home remained the same. A bedroom, a living room, a small kitchen – a simple apartment about twelve pyeong in size, sparsely furnished with only a bed, a small vanity table, a wardrobe, and a table and chair set. Many lifetimes ago, she'd lived in a large, elaborately decorated mansion, but the space had only amplified her loneliness.

She made it a point to have a job in each of her lives, and because she barely spent any money, her wealth naturally grew. Ironically, she found herself having fewer needs and wants. She walked listlessly over to the window.

'How beautiful.'

Chapter II

MARIGOLD

She had chosen this neighbourhood for its name: Marigold. To think there was a place named after her mother's favourite flower! She contemplated her surroundings with a bursting heart. Her house appeared to sit atop a hill, above a cluster of red-brick houses bunched together like flowers. The delicious aroma of cooking rice permeated the alleyways. She imagined it to be a serene neighbourhood, where the sun would dip peacefully below the horizon and silently rise again. She could see scattered lights from the other houses and smoke spiralling from their chimneys.

Standing in silence, she took in the scenery. There was no mad bustle of people in the streets, but the place didn't seem forlorn either. Still holding her cup, she slid open the glass door and stepped out on to the veranda. The cold tiles tickled her bare feet.

With her back to the sea, she let the wind caress her face.

Glancing to her left, she gasped. The setting sun was using its remaining strength to paint the sky a fiery red. Across the ocean, the flaming sphere slowly bowed its way out.

Have sunsets always been this breathtaking?

The village was nestled at the foot of a mountain, flanked by the ocean on two sides and a city on the other two. Closing her eyes, she drew a deep breath; saltiness pricked her throat. A wave of sadness crept up on her, and suddenly, hot tears began to spill from her eyes.

'How is this sunset so gorgeous? There really is still beauty in the world.'

She wiped away her tears as if she didn't want to be caught crying. A gentle breeze carrying a floral scent tickled her nose. She tucked away the flyaway strands of her hair, her eyes reflecting the sun's orange glow.

'Mmm. What's that smell?'

She inhaled deeply, and something in the depths of her memory stirred. Where had she known this smell? Thoughts swirling, she sipped her now lukewarm water. As the last embers of the sun disappeared over the horizon, a crimson sheen lingered over the sky.

Darkness didn't fall immediately. The sun continued to radiate light, and even after it had gone under, its glow remained. *Light and darkness aren't two sides of a coin; they form a continuum.* She gazed at the dimming landscape. *Even in the darkest spaces, there is light.*

Little by little, the moon began to reveal itself, adding a shimmer to the black sky. *Perhaps we fail to notice the morning moon because we're only ever looking for the sun.* She decided to stay up all night and sat there, hugging her knees. Darkness might seem to last for eternity, but day would always break. *Perhaps the only thing we never have to work for is the morning, which comes around to greet us every day.*

'In life, nothing is forever. Not the darkness, nor the light.'

A cluster of images flitted through her mind. Of how in her past lives she used to offer healing tea to the people she met. How the darkness they'd been trapped in gradually lifted as they drank, and like the rising sun, they raised their heads, a smile lighting up their faces.

'It . . . it's all coming back . . .'

Clink!

The cup slipped through her fingers, and white shards flew. Why was she remembering that last night with her parents now? Her hands flew up to her mouth even though it was the crack of dawn and nobody was around to hear her if she screamed. Her dad's voice rang in her ears – the latter part of his words she thought she'd missed.

'And for both her powers to blossom fully, she first needs to hone her gift for comforting and healing before tapping into her second power – the power to make dreams come true. And isn't the latter also about helping others in need? There are so few who possess this power. It's rare and precious. The power chose her.'

Why? Why only now? Drained of the energy to cry, her feet gripped the ground as she willed herself to disappear from the face of the Earth. Slowly, her body started to fade away. Behind her, the sun continued to rise, dutifully carrying out its daily task.

'Urgh . . . my head . . . it hurts. Why am I not vanishing?'

She had only managed to transfer herself inside. She clenched her fists and watched as the shards on the floor transformed into white petals and winged their way out of the window, soaring into the sky. The petals inserted themselves into the gaps between the clouds and cleared them away to allow the dazzling sunlight to shine, unfiltered, into the room where she stood stock still. Against a brilliant blue, the sun blazed, and in an instant her outfit morphed into a black satin dress adorned with petals from the red camellia flower.

Her eyes flew open and her ponytail loosened, sending her long hair billowing towards the window. Today was that kind of day, against the night's quiet bleakness before the incoming storm.

'The way the sun burns and sets the sky on fire feels as though every sunset here is the last. As if there's no tomorrow.'

For the past few days, she had sat down in the same spot by the window, watching the sun rise and dip beyond the horizon. Today, she finally stepped outside. How could it have taken her so long to recall the last memory of the most painful day in her life? The bitterness ate at her, but now that she knew, she couldn't sit around and do nothing. This wasn't the time for resentment or self-reproach. Instead, she should face the problem head-on. Surely there would be an answer in the end?

Right now, what she needed was a place that would allow her to focus on healing and helping others.

In this place called Marigold.

'Aigoo, are you helping your daughter take care of her kids? All three of them? Have you eaten?'

'Yeah, but they've gone back home for the weekend. I'll take some of that fish cake.'

The residents greeted each other and along the street piping-hot food in black plastic bags and thousand-won notes changed hands. It seemed like everyone in this quaint neighbourhood had lived here their whole lives. It wouldn't surprise her if they knew the exact number of spoons in each of their neighbours' kitchens.

'The kimbap is on the house.'

'What? Who gives kimbap for free when all I have bought is some fish cake? Are you even earning anything? Here, take the money.'

'Aigoo, no, no, you keep it. You can come by again tomorrow.'

The friendly banter was making her strangely hungry. It had been a long time since she'd felt like eating anything. She headed in the direction of the voices and stepped into an old restaurant called Our Snack Shop.

The space was so tiny, there was only room for a few red tables, which were covered with grease stains so ancient that even a good wipe would not make them less sticky. Resisting the urge to correct the spelling mistakes on the menu, she ordered a roll of kimbap.

When was the last time I had a proper meal? In my previous lifetime, or was it way before that? I'm pretty sure I haven't eaten since I woke up here.

For a woman on a mission, eating and enjoying food felt like a luxury she didn't have time for. She usually relied on special pills; just one would be enough to sustain her throughout the day. She had inherited the formula from a dying acquaintance in one of her past lives, whose face, by now, had become a blur among her memories. Having long forgotten how to chew or swallow food, she stared at the plate set down in front of her.

'Even if you aren't in the mood to eat, push it down,' said the owner. 'Else you'll snap into two! I didn't have an appetite today either, but I forced it down. Tough, but I managed. That'll keep your stomach going. Or your appetite will just keep shrinking.'

When was the last time someone had told her to eat well? How many lives ago was that? She mechanically pushed a piece of the kimbap into her mouth. Her eyes landed on the ajumma's belly, the fraying edges of the floral apron stretched over it, and she tilted her head in thought.

Is it because I haven't eaten in a while? I can't really taste anything.

The ajumma set down a piping-hot bowl of fish cake soup in front of her.

'Agasshi, what's your name?'

At this question, she paused her mental count of the floating pieces of spring onion and pepper in the soup and instead let her eyes fall on a yellow leaflet lying on the next table with the words: JIEUN MART. She continued to chew the kimbap in silence, before slowly moving her lips.

'Jieun.'

'Jieunnie? What a pretty name. All right, enjoy the kimbap and come again to try the ramyeon!'

Jieun. A pretty name indeed. *Jieunnie* – a person who writes stories. A little smile turned up the corners of her mouth as she slurped a spoonful of the hot soup with the floating bits.

How comforting.

The young woman – no, Jieun – swallowed the kimbap before speaking.

'Ajumma, how much does this building cost?' She spoke informally to the older lady. 'I want to buy it.'

'What? You want to buy the entire building? Do you know what you're saying? Agasshi, do you have lots of money?'

'Um . . . I guess you could say that.'

'Oho! Your family is rich?'

'How much money do I need to be considered rich? I worked hard to earn it, but I lost interest in spending any and naturally I have quite a bit saved up. Anyway, let me know who owns the building. Tell them I'll pay triple the asking price. And I'll cut your rent in half and never raise it.'

'Aigoo, you really are rich! Pretty in looks, and pretty in heart. All right, buy it if you can! It's no trouble giving you a phone number. Here you go!'

Jieun looked at the string of numbers scrawled on the yellowed memo paper and broke into a huge smile.

'Ajumma, I'll cut the rent, but in return, you make sure the food stays the same. No new menu or any extra items. Don't ever change it.'

'Aha! Here's a missy who knows a person's worth. My food

is good, eh? But agasshi, why are you speaking so informally to me when we've only just met?'

'I'm older than I look. In fact, I've lived much longer than you.'

'OK, I'll take your word for it.'

Taking in Jieun's solemn expression, her pale face and the long wavy black hair that fell to her waist, the ajumma gave a chuckle. In her eyes, Jieun could pass for a twenty-something, yet from certain angles, she looked like she could be in her forties, too. When she first saw Jieun standing in front of the eatery, gazing into the distance with empty, forlorn eyes, her heart went out to her. The woman's stick-thin limbs made her want to give her a big hug, and that was perhaps why she'd deliberately raised her voice, in the hope that the young lady would take it as an invitation to come in.

'Agasshi – no, Jieun. Where did you buy your dress? I love it. It'd look great on me.'

The ajumma placed her fingers on the pink floral apron draped over her own belly and stared wistfully at Jieun's black dress with the red flower pattern. Jieun's eyes lingered on the ajumma's wrinkled hands and gnarled knuckles, and she felt a pang in her chest as a memory surfaced.

'Mummy, what if we don't have a heart?'

'Hmm? Then we wouldn't be able to feel anything – not love, not happiness and not sadness.'

'But isn't it a good thing not to be sad?'

'Did something make you sad?'

'No, but I read about sadness and pain, and I'm curious.'

'If your heart is aching, how about taking it out, washing it clean and airing it in the sun? You'll feel much more refreshed the next day.'

'You can take a heart out?'

'Well, if you can't, how about drawing your feelings on paper?'

'Oooh, I'll do that. But if I'm feeling upset, Mummy, you can just hug me,' said the child, looking up with trusting eyes.

Instead of answering, her mum rubbed her back and patted her lightly. She pulled out a cookie from her apron and held it out to the child. As she nibbled on it, crumbs clung to her rosy cheeks. Spreading her arms out in her yellow dress, she zoomed around, pretending to fly. Just then, the wind stirred up a trail of petals. The young girl danced around in the sea of red before turning into petals and disappearing.

She looked down at her dress. 'I bought this about fifty centuries ago. I don't think it can be found anywhere now. See you next time, ajumma.'

Concealing her sadness beneath her long lashes, Jieun looked away from the ajumma's apron, pulling herself out of her memory. She paid for the food and took a final look around the shop before stepping out. Standing in the street, she breathed out slowly. Then she got her phone and tapped in the building owner's number. As she waited for the call to connect, she noticed a fading sign hanging next door.

MIND LAUNDRY
Luxury Dry Cleaning.
We remove all types of stains.

She mouthed each word carefully, piecing together the missing letters where some of the stickers had peeled off.

'Mmm, a laundry service . . . Stain removal . . . I wonder if they could do anything about the ones we all have on our hearts?'

Computerized Cleaning.
Fully equipped with the newest machines.

'Newest? How is this *new*?'

She took a walk around the long-abandoned laundry shop, a look of determination coming over her. Just as ironing smooths crumpled clothes, would it also work on the creases in people's feelings? What if stains on the heart could be removed like those on a shirt? Would that make a person wholly happy again? A light flickered on in Jieun's dark eyes.

It feels so possible here.

She closed her eyes to focus, her solemn expression gradually relaxing.

Behind her, night fell. As it always did.

Some feelings can be easily smoothed, but certain marks in our hearts are better left untouched. There is also the matter of any hearts that have been torn, those that need mending before they can be washed, and those darker stains that will dye the laundry water grey no matter how vigorously they are scrubbed and rinsed.

Jieun imagined a safe space for these hearts, drawing inspiration from the places she herself had felt the most at ease. Places where she had experienced heartfelt conversations. Places filled with cherished memories of her favourite people. A few came to mind. Aunt Chunbok's two-storey house by the lake, the living room at Uncle Yeongsu's, which looked out to sea, Grandma Sophie's garden tucked away in the countryside of Europe. Her thoughts turned back to laundry. For it to dry properly, ample sunlight would be essential.

I'd better build a place facing the sun.

Of the places that came to mind, she had the most vivid memories of Grandma Sophie's house, which had a stream of visitors all day long. Centuries-old trees stood majestically in the garden, and in the shade of their large canopies the neighbours gathered to share food and stories.

Perhaps I could make a place like that? People would be free to come and go; it could be a sanctuary that provided shade and shelter. Deep in thought, she didn't realize a smile was playing on her lips.

She closed her eyes and began to dream.

A two-storey house took shape in her mind, built from walnut wood, strong and sturdy, next to a garden that bloomed all year round. The exterior referenced European architecture, but what if on the inside, she added rafters, like the ones in traditional hanoks?

'May customers walk out feeling stronger. Just as trees grow more resilient every year, I hope they will return home with a growth ring around their hearts.'

She imagined walking up seven wooden steps to an arched entrance surrounded by red camellias in full bloom. When she pushed the ancient door open, it would feel as if she'd entered a secret garden, a brand-new world.

'Since the house is at the top of the hill, let it bask in warm sunlight in the day, and at night, may it be illuminated by the glow of the moon.'

In the wee hours of the night, when everyone was sleeping soundly in bed, the mind laundry slowly blossomed into existence amid swirls of crimson light. Like a flower bud unfolding petal by petal, the structure stretched upwards and outwards, until it became the exact replica of the two-storey building Jieun had imagined.

On the ground floor was the reception, where the laundry would be taken in, and the tall bar table would double up as a kitchen space to brew and serve Jieun's special tea. Up the stairs was the laundry room, its decor kept simple. After all, it was a space where stains of the heart would be removed and wrinkled feelings ironed. She made space for the washing machines and set up the ironing corner, not forgetting to include a rest area with two tables that could comfortably seat four each.

'Oh yes, the lighting.'

She installed warm yellow lights and dimmed them, creating an inviting atmosphere for honest conversations. Instead of glaring lights that would throw the visitors' faces and expressions into stark relief, the gentle glow would shade their feelings and put them at ease.

In the corner, she put in a steel spiral staircase, with just enough space for one person at a time to climb up. The winding steps led to a rooftop garden, where clothes lines had been hung up.

In her past lives, on days when she'd shared in the pain of others, Jieun would return home to do her laundry and contemplate their stories. She would add the detergent and scrub until the tub was brimming with foamy bubbles. As she rinsed her clothes, any dust and dirt would be washed off together with the bubbles and soap. Then she'd give the clothes a good shake down before hanging them up, all the while thinking how great it would be if sadness and pain could be washed away as thoroughly. Gazing at the washing as it dripped water on to the ground, she felt as though the sludge of negativity in the world were drying out, too. Whenever she put her heart into doing laundry, the gloom on the faces of the people around her would clear up like a cloudless blue sky.

'May those who walk through these doors feel refreshed,' Jieun spoke her wish aloud.

Buoyed by her earnest desire to create a space that would comfort and heal, atop the highest hill in the neighbourhood, the Marigold Mind Laundry came to be.

'Phew.'

Jieun opened her eyes and looked up at the building. She'd been afraid that her second power, of making wishes come true, would fail her. After all, no matter how desperate she had been, her wish to grow old and die had never worked. To be stuck in a relentless cycle of rebirths, in a body that would never become old, was a pain that rivalled the loss of her family. Even in the life she'd been living just before this one, despite trying her hardest to dream, nothing had happened. Was she being blessed with another power in this life?

She let out a tiny sigh.

One, two, three, four, five, six, seven.

She placed her foot carefully on each wooden step and walked steadily up, stopping at the door. The whirlwind of petals that had conjured up her new Mind Laundry still swirled around at her feet before vanishing into the patterns on her dress.

In the silence of the night, Jieun placed her hand on the door, pushed it open and turned on the lights. Just as she'd imagined, the space was filled with a warm glow. She took a deep breath. Inhaling the earthy scent of wood, she felt the ears of her heart slowly opening. Murmurs of strangers' innermost thoughts seemed to drift towards her. She listened before heading to the kitchen.

It had been a while, but today, she would put her heart and soul into brewing her unique healing tea that would iron out the smallest of wrinkles, easing the drinker's mind. In the quiet hours, somewhere out there was a person who craved its comfort.

Or perhaps I'm the one who needs it more tonight.

Chapter III

JAEHA

'If only I could take out my mind, wash it thoroughly, and stick it back in,' Yeonhee muttered as she walked up the steep staircase.

It was May, an achingly beautiful season when the landscape shimmered in a lush green and the scent of flowers floated on the balmy night-time breeze.

'How would you even do that? Take out your mind?'

Jaeha sounded slightly breathless as he adjusted the back-pack straps that cut into his shoulders under the weight of his laptop. Did the mind even have a shape? If so, he, too, would love to see and touch it.

'I said, *if only*. Wouldn't we be happier if we could shed all these painful memories? It's precisely because our minds are unwell that we keep trapping ourselves in unhappy thoughts. Yet we still go about our lives – working, eating, meeting friends – as if everything's fine. Just as I'm smiling but crumbling on the inside. If only the pain were gone, maybe life would feel possible again.'

Yeonhee stopped halfway up the steps, catching her breath. She would love to breathe in warm air and release the cold in her, but sadly, the opposite was happening. Even something this simple wasn't going her way.

'You know what? Our minds can also show signs of wear over time. Mine's worn so thin that it might disappear at any moment.'

'Yeah, I get you. What's the point of living anyway? It's all meaningless.'

Jaeha wondered why he existed at all. What was it like to love life, to feel as though every day held something hopeful? He would love to experience that for once.

'I get out of bed because my eyes are open and I keep going because I'm alive. Don't you feel the same?'

Jaeha took out a strand of dried squid from a snack pack stuffed in his bag and popped it into his mouth, his eyes squinting to a line as he looked up at the night sky. He counted the stars as he worked his jaw.

Yeonhee tilted her head to the side. She had a quote by Paul Valéry in her head.

The wind is rising. We must try to live.

'If the passing wind could be a reason to live, why are we finding life so difficult?' Halfway up the steps, under the flickering glow of the streetlight below, Jaeha and Yeonhee sat elbow to elbow, each absorbed in the quiet darkness of the night.

'The sky is clear, but the moon is hiding.'

Feeling the chill seeping out of the concrete steps, Jaeha

stuffed his hands under his bottom. Life was as sharp as his bones jutting against the cold cement, but at least he could now feel the palm-sized warmth of his hands.

'Hey, look. What's that?'

Jaeha stood up with a jerk, pulling Yeonhee up with him. They grasped each other's shoulders, staring wide-eyed ahead. The same thought crossed their minds.

Have we finally gone mad?

Swirling in endless circles above them were red flowers – camellias – that seemed to hover around the old snack shop at the top of the steps. Upon a closer look, the clusters of camellias were circling in the space beside it, and in the eye of the whirlpool, a building was rising.

'It's blooming, the building . . .'

'Oh my god, you're right.'

'Are we dreaming?'

'Really? You mean we're having this conversation in our dreams?'

That seemed like a beautiful moment, too, being sucked hand in hand into a whirlpool of petals. Sweat glistened on their clasped palms. A two-storey building, which looked sort of like a house, was flowering into existence amid a whirlwind of fluttering petals. It was a shocking sight to see planks of wood rising in between them.

'Jaeha . . . that house. It's always been there – hasn't it?'

Yeonhee rubbed her eyes.

'Not that I know of.'

'Has life become so tough that we're losing our marbles?'

'Maybe.'

'Let's go.'

'Huh?'

'Let's check it out.'

'Uh—'

Yeonhee pulled Jaeha with her and climbed up the steps. Sometimes a second can feel like a thousand years. When they stood in front of the old sign, it felt as though an eternity had passed.

Yeonhee read out the words on the sign.

'Mind . . . Laundry?'

'Look how old the sign is. It must've been here for ages.'

'Yeah, but how did we not notice it?'

MIND LAUNDRY
Luxury Dry Cleaning.
We remove all types of stains.

Jaeha looked at the faded letter-stickers, torn in several places. He turned his head. To the right was Our Snack Shop, looking exactly as he remembered it. Pressing his nose against its window, he cupped his hands around his temples and peered into the dark interior. The grease-stained tables, the mess of cooking foil, the ajumma owner's condiment set, which she used liberally. And even a pile of unsold fritters, which must have turned soggy by now.

'Even without any other restaurant in the neighbourhood, I don't ever eat the kimbap here unless I'm literally starving,' muttered Jaeha. 'No idea how it can be so flavourless even with all that seasoning.'

Together, they took three steps back and looked up at the building. *It is! No, it isn't. It isn't. Yes, it is!* On a moonless night, those who believe that *it is*, might turn out to be right. After all, there are moments in life when a wish, if desperate enough, might bend reality to our hopes.

The two of them stood slack-jawed at this building that had appeared out of nowhere. The wind blew, and they caught a waft of floral scent and the lush smell of garden.

A piece of paper floating on the wind appeared from nowhere; Yeonhee quickly caught it. As she read the text, her heart gave a squeeze. With the other hand, she rubbed circles on her chest to soothe herself.

We remove stains from the heart and mind,
and erase your painful memories.

If it makes you happier,
we can also iron out any creases,
and get rid of unwanted blotches.

We remove all types of stains.
Welcome to the Marigold Mind Laundry.

Yours sincerely,
The Owner

'You know what, Jaeha? If only I could erase the memories of Heejae, I think I'd be able to smile again.'

Jaeha glanced up. Yeonhee's eyes were closed; she was

taking deep breaths. He slung an arm over her shoulder, holding the other corner of the leaflet as he read. He, too, closed his eyes.

'If only we could get rid of what's hurting us . . . Would it mean that we can finally find happiness?'

There was a creak as the door of the laundry swung open. The choice was now theirs. Go with the flow of this strange night, or turn back home?

They stepped forwards at the same time.

'Welcome.'

Jieun stifled a yawn and greeted her visitors. She had been about to doze off when she sensed their presence and came down the stairs. Or rather, she had materialized from thin air. From their expressions, she had given them quite a shock. Running her fingers through her long black hair, Jieun gestured for them to join her at the bar table.

'Did I scare you? I wanted to walk but this has become a habit. Glad I got the tea ready. Come, take a seat and have a cup.'

Yeonhee and Jaeha stared at her awkwardly. A moment ago, they had been mulling over the leaflet; the next second, the door had swung open and, now, here was a strange woman who'd appeared out of nowhere to offer them tea. Jaeha couldn't help but think back to his wrongdoings in life, although he didn't think there was anything that deserved death. But if he hadn't stumbled upon the afterlife, was he hallucinating?

'Don't worry, we're a laundry service. You walked in after seeing our leaflet, right? I wrote that myself. I must say, I do have a knack for writing. Come on, stop gaping and sit down.'

Jieun steeped the healing tea in a white porcelain teapot and looked expectantly at them. She could read their sadness, feel their pain. As she poured, she tried to gauge how big a stain she might have to remove. Hopefully all they needed was some light ironing.

Yeonhee took the proffered cup and sat down. She wondered how old the woman was. Twenty-something? Thirty? Perhaps she was even in her forties. One side of her profile put her at her twenties, but from the other side, there was something wizened about her features. She looked sad and even though she spoke to them as if she already knew them, which some might find rude, Yeonhee found her strangely endearing. The woman looked and sounded aloof, yet there was a warmth about her. So strange . . . Where had she seen this woman before? Yeonhee wondered if she was from the neighbourhood. Judging from her stick-thin limbs, it didn't seem like she'd been eating. Her footsteps were light, delicate, reminding Yeonhee of gliding petals. She wasn't the type anyone would usually call a beauty, but there was no denying that she radiated charisma. Or was that part of being beautiful? One thing for sure, she was an enigmatic presence.

Sneaking glances at her, Yeonhee picked up the cup, her hands trembling slightly as she took a sip, and then another. She began to ease up. Jaeha was still standing, so she pulled him to a chair and signalled to him with her eyes to drink his tea. Having grown up together, they didn't need words to understand each other.

Try the tea.

Aren't you worried that it's spiked?

Who cares? What can be worse than our lives right now?

True.

Jaeha swung his backpack on to the table and sat down.

As they sipped quietly, they took a leisurely look around them. From the outside, the laundry had reminded them of a café you might see in the Provençal countryside, but the hanok-inspired interior gave off a calming vibe. The building had exerted a mysterious pull on them, but they were so glad they'd come in. Moonlight was filtering through a huge skylight. Wait. When did the moon appear? They certainly hadn't noticed it a minute ago.

'It's night-time, yet somehow, with all the moonlight streaming in, it feels like one of those slow-moving summer days. This is such a warm and cosy place.'

Yeonhee walked over to the bookshelf and bent down to inspect the potted plants, the fanning leaves and tiny blades that meshed so harmoniously with the room's atmosphere.

The solid wood furniture added to the calming vibes. She picked up her teacup again, catching on its side the reflection of a sliver of moon, like a landscape painting of water. Yeonhee looked over at Jieun, her eyes brimming with curiosity.

'Is this really a laundry service?'

'Mm, it is. We don't charge cleaning fees, but you'll owe a debt of gratitude to be paid thereafter.'

'Debt?' Yeonhee looked alarmed. 'I have enough on my plate . . . I can't even pay off my student loans.'

'Not that kind of debt. I believe there's a stain you wish to remove, or a crease you want ironed out? After I've supported you with that, freed you from your pain, you'll meet someone one day who's having a hard time. Offer your help without asking for anything in return. That'll be the cleaning fee you owe.'

'You don't look like an angel from a fairy tale, but you're acting like one,' Jaeha mused, chuckling.

Yeonhee shot Jaeha a glare. She turned her attention back to Jieun, who was taking two white t-shirts from a drawer. Some people had the uncanny ability to make others feel comfortable, and this woman, totally unknown to her just a short while ago, was having that effect on her. So peculiar. What a strange night.

'Here, take one t-shirt each. If you feel the thing that has been hurting you for a long time has formed a crust on your heart, or if there are creases that you wish to iron out, put on the t-shirt. But be warned. Once you take it off, the memories will also vanish. So think carefully. Are you really OK with erasing those memories?'

'If the mark hurts so much, then isn't it better not to remember? Why hold on to the misery?'

Jaeha accepted the t-shirt respectfully with both hands. Jieun's eyes were dark and inscrutable. Instead of replying, she lowered her gaze and simply shook her head. She walked over to the large window flanking the room and looked up at the night sky.

'If you're not miserable, does that mean everything is good?'

'Isn't that the same as being happy?'

'I mean, if we take away any suffering, is happiness all that's left?'

'Uhm . . . isn't it?'

'Over the course of a single day, do you only feel happy or miserable?'

'Of course not! How can life be made up of only those two emotions?'

'Then, what else do you feel?'

'Uhm. Sleepy. Irritated. Hungry. Unmotivated. Wanting to go back home even though I'm already at home. Sometimes, if I really want to feel like I'm alive, I chew some squid. I keep on chewing, but the squid remains tough – like my life. I keep going, but it never breaks. And my jaw starts to ache and the next moment I'm like, "Screw this!" I get pissed off. And that's when I feel like I'm alive. Funny, isn't it? . . . I don't even know if this is misery or happiness any more.'

Jaeha paused, flustered at spilling his guts in such a rapid-fire rap. Other than to Yeonhee, he had never shared his true feelings with anyone, choosing instead to mask them behind a bubbly persona. There's a saying that you don't throw stones at people who smile, so even when he found everyone annoying and hated them all, he still plastered on a smile. As for what happiness was, he had no idea. His motto in life was that if he had to be miserable, better less than more. Why was it that today, here he was pouring his heart out to a woman he'd never met before in his life?

'Just as there are heartbreaking memories that need to be erased if you want to move forward, there is also the pain that is a kind of fuel that keeps you going. Sadness can sometimes give you strength.'

Jieun's words were plain, but Jaeha, who had been staring blankly at the t-shirt, suddenly gulped down a large mouthful of tea and pulled the t-shirt over his head. When was the last time he had truly smiled? He couldn't remember. Yeonhee gazed at him for a moment. She closed her eyes. Tonight was one of those moments. No matter what was said, the memories would surface by themselves – never forgotten, only that we had chosen to look away.

After a few awkward moments, Jieun said, 'What is it? A stain you want to remove, or a crease you want to iron?'

Jaeha lowered his head. Whether it was a stain or a crease, whether it should be removed or ironed, he had not the slightest idea.

Jieun looked at the young man, so still and inscrutable, then she stood up and headed towards the stairs.

'Finish up your tea and follow me.'

'. . . OK.'

Jaeha drank up his tea and glanced at Yeonhee. She took out a book from the backpack, flipped to a random page and started reading while Jaeha followed the woman up the stairs to the first floor.

By the window stood two huge washing machines and in the corner was a silver sewing machine and next to that, an ironing board. Even with all these industrial appliances, the space felt more like a café, thanks to the solid wood furniture and warm lighting. Jaeha spotted the rest area and sank into the sofa.

'Close your eyes and concentrate on the memories you want to get rid of, and they'll manifest as stains on your white t-shirt. Before you take it off, think carefully about whether you're truly all right with removing those memories. The choice, the consequences and the responsibility are all yours.'

'And after I take it off, what happens?'

'Just trust me. I'll wash it clean for you,' Jieun said, waving her hands in the direction of the washing machines.

There were many ways to remove a smear, but letting her visitors choose to put a stained piece of clothing into the washing machine was a small gesture of consideration on her part. After all, it was a laundry service. She could have chosen to erase their pains with the healing tea and by listening to their stories, as she had done in her past lives, but she thought it was important to give them the time and space to decide if the stain was something they really wanted removed. Perhaps they'd prefer to keep it close to their heart after all.

'Once the machine stops running, the stain will be washed off. It'll be as if that incident had never happened, and that moment in your life will be erased. You might feel better without it, but there are also times you may want to cherish. So, think carefully. Often, we don't know whether what we have is good or bad until we've lost it.'

Jieun tried to keep her footsteps quiet as she moved towards the spiral staircase, leaving Jaeha sitting with his eyes closed. She went outside to the rooftop and looked up. She could tell the time just by watching the light in the sky. The moon was the oldest of clocks.

'It pains me to see people wearing a bright smile all day long. Nobody can smile all the time. They smile only because they believe that life can only go on if their sadness is veiled. But sometimes the pain must be wiped away for them to breathe freely again,' she muttered.

Thinking of Jaeha and the permanent smile etched on his face, Jieun folded her arms and closed her eyes. Taking a deep breath, she spread her arms out wide, as though wings would sprout out from her back, ready to take off.

In the shadows, a watchful eye stared at her from behind.

–Had your lunch, Ms Yeonja? Don't forget to eat and don't work too hard!–

Jaeha texted his mother – she made side dishes at a restaurant catering for taxi drivers – before slipping his phone back into his pocket. He took a long stretch. He had been barricading himself in his rented basement room, editing a movie he'd shot three months earlier. He would keep at it until exhaustion took over, and when he woke up starving he'd wolf down some ramyeon before returning to work. Today was the first time in a while that he had stepped out for some sun. He rubbed his scraggly beard and tried to flatten the mess of hair tickling the nape of his neck. Shifting his baseball cap, he squeezed one eye shut and squinted up at the sun. *How dazzling*. Looking up at the sky was the quickest way he knew to make himself feel better. He could lift his head anytime, anywhere to enjoy its vastness without spending a single won. The sky was always overhead. But it also knew to maintain a comfortable distance – not too near, not too far.

'Awfully blue sky today. Well, not *awful*. I should say *awesomely* blue.'

He turned his eyes away from the sky and headed for the convenience store thirty metres down the street.

He remembered this stage in his life so vividly. He'd quit a four-year engineering college degree to enrol at an arts school. When a short film he made for his graduation project received a prize at a small European festival, he was touted as a rising star and debuted to great fanfare. His professors and classmates had had high hopes for him; the media lauded him as a young, upcoming director to watch out for. His experimental take on the theme of existentialism had earned him the praise 'post-Park Chan-wook' and all eyes were on him for his next big hit. He'd even scored the occasional invite to appear on TV. Jaeha had lapped up the attention, feeling like the world was his oyster.

However, after that initial success, he got stuck in a long dry spell. He needed his next film to dazzle, but there was a problem: the script. He had yet to write a single word. He couldn't even nail down a theme. His mind remained stubbornly blank. For the next two years, he'd lived off his mother's tiny wages before he finally took on a couple of odd jobs, mostly at construction sites or doing deliveries. He couldn't be selfish any more, not when he saw how Ms Yeonja was still heading to the restaurant after her knee surgery, popping three painkillers in one go. Gradually, he scrimped enough to rent a basement room to focus on filmmaking again. By this point, five years had passed since his award-winning short.

Bzzz. As he sat down to lunch – a dosirak-style ready meal with seven side dishes – his phone vibrated. Seated at the plastic table outside the convenience store, he gulped down a beer and checked Ms Yeonja's text. *Kyaaa – nothing beats daytime drinking.*

–OK – I'll be able to rest easy after you find a job and get married.–

'Hey hey, Ms Yeonja. It's not that easy to find a job *and* a wife. I want to make something of myself, too. Just wait. Once my movie hits it big this time, I'll make sure you live in luxury!'

The gusto in his voice was his promise to Ms Yeonja and a cry to the world. As he eased open the plastic cover of the dosirak, he jiggled his shoulders in a dance. Shovelling rice into his mouth, he broke into a broad grin as he envisioned what lay ahead.

'Young man! I always see you pulling a long face but what a chipper mood you're in today. Have a good lunch!'

It was the convenience store owner, an ajusshi who had apparently worked for a major conglomerate before his retirement. As he cleared the table, he glanced at Jaeha.

'I've eaten my share of convenience store dosiraks,' said Jaeha, 'but the ones here are unbeatable. Ajusshi, have you taken your lunch?'

'I'll eat when it's time to clear out the expired dosiraks. No good to let unsold food go to waste. Would you like an extra one, young man?'

'I'm good today, thanks. But don't keep eating expired food. You have to take care of yourself!'

'Convenience store food isn't as unhealthy as people used to say. Look. Our dosiraks are low in sodium and full of the five essential nutrients our body needs! Are you sure you don't want one more?'

'Wow, you're right. There's even a low-sodium label here. On second thoughts, sure, I'll have another one, please!'

Jaeha bought two instant cup noodles and the owner packed a just-expired dosirak into his plastic bag. He made his way back to his room, ready for another intense spell of editing. It was his first project after the award-winning short, so he really wanted to live up to the expectations weighing on him. But nothing ever seemed to work out the way he wanted. It is often said that life is like a pendulum – swinging between good and bad. But for Jaeha, life was a bell struck only from the side of misfortune, ringing loud and clear.

'You call this a movie?'

'What the hell was the director thinking?'

'Absolute waste of time and money.'

His movie, screened at two small art theatres in Seoul, opened to abysmal reviews. Despite submitting his work to all the overseas film festivals, he failed to make the preliminary cut for a single one. His friends and acquaintances comforted him, saying that his film had cinematic quality, but in their eyes he could see everything they had left unspoken.

*

Then a new memory came to the surface. Why, of all things, was he suddenly reminded of the hem of his father's dark jeans? If only the man he'd called *Father* had fulfilled his role, Jaeha wouldn't have needed to resort to odd jobs and could have channelled all his energy into filmmaking. The least that man could have done was to send some money. No. Jaeha should never have quit engineering college in the first place. He should have kept filmmaking as a hobby and not made it his vocation. If only he'd followed Ms Yeonja's advice to apply for a desk job at a conglomerate or study for the civil service exam . . . No . . . What if he hadn't joined an advertising agency after his movie flopped? Maybe he would have been better off as a YouTube producer . . . Or would it have been better if he had never been born . . .

Excuses flashed through his mind – excuses for becoming the failure he was.

But his deepest and darkest pain had been when he was a young boy. The days of being made to huddle at home alone in the dark, waiting for Ms Yeonja to return from work in the small hours of the night, watching movies to stave off the fear and loneliness.

'Which of those stains would you like to erase?'

Every one of us is born with a heart as soft and supple as a baby's bottom, but in life, a scrape here and a bump there leaves behind marks. The stains multiply on top of each other, occasionally forming creases. Over time, some blemishes might fade, just as wrinkles sometimes smooth out on their own. But there are occasions when the longer we hold on to them, the more likely it is that they will fester into wounds or even leave something like an ache or a gaping hole behind.

The painfully bright smile plastered across Jaeha's cheeks reminded Jieun of the two faces of the moon. His eyes were saying 'I could die for all I care', but it would take an understanding person to recognize his look. Which was why Jieun had paid particular attention to him from the moment he'd stepped inside the door. The stains on his heart probably numbered more than a few. Muttering to herself as if in prayer, she scuttled back downstairs to the washing machines. As she'd expected, there were several blotches on Jaeha's t-shirt.

'Can you remove them all?'

Hearing Jieun's footsteps, Jaeha awkwardly took off the t-shirt he'd layered on top of his clothes. He'd thought he'd be fine as long as he kept up the pretence, but he wasn't fine. At the sight of the patches staining the white shirt, Jaeha was both shocked and conflicted.

After his movie had flopped, Jaeha had found a contract role at an advertising agency and was already in his fifth year there. Every year, the CEO would tell him, 'Let's get you switched over to a permanent position,' but somehow that instruction never seemed to make it to the HR department. Now aged thirty-three, Jaeha was desperate to break free of the grind of semi-basement rentals and contract jobs. Even when he managed to get himself a girlfriend, the thought of laying bare the circumstances of his life to someone else bothered him so much that whenever a relationship was on the cusp of turning serious, he would push the woman away. He started opting for casual flings – fleeting, no strings attached.

Which stain should he remove first? Jaeha mulled it over.

'You can't just erase your whole life. You're thinking that everything will be a bed of roses if you can start all over again, right?'

'H-how did you know?'

Jaeha scratched his head in embarrassment and avoided Jieun's gaze, fingering the t-shirt instead. He was indeed wondering if a clean slate could bring happiness. And who was this woman anyway, who claimed to be able to wash the marks off a pained heart? She had to be his age at most. But her eyes were deep and sad, as if she had lived a thousand years. Yet there was kindness in them, too. He could feel the warmth radiating from her sad look.

Jaeha liked to observe people's eyes. It was easy to lie with words, but the eyes always spoke the truth. Like how someone could say *I love you*, but their gaze was cold. Or *I'm so tired*, but you could see how much they were loving life. Or when someone said *believe me*, but not a single ounce of truth showed in their eyes. Whenever she'd said, *I'll be back, wait for me*, Ms Yeonja's eyes had brimmed with the saddest of sadness. But Jaeha hadn't seen any melancholy in her eyes in a long time – not since she'd started studying again, enjoying the courses at the online university.

'Just erase one. If you get rid of everything, what's there left in life . . . ? Wounds are also a part of you. Just take out the most painful one.' Jieun's gaze was steady. Her eyes and words merged into one.

Jaeha trembled as a shudder ran through him. 'I'd like to erase the loneliness.'

'Loneliness?'

'Yes . . . the loneliness I felt whenever Ms Yeonja locked the door behind her.'

The details were lost among his memories, but he was about three or four years old when, one day, the man he'd called Father left home and never returned. The man's face was now a blur, but Jaeha still vividly remembered the hem of the jeans he'd tried to hold on to. The colour of the fabric, the roughness of its touch as the figure stood unmoving, neither reaching out to hug Jaeha nor pulling away, despite the little boy wailing at him not to leave, his tiny fists creasing the fabric.

After that man was gone, Jaeha and his mother had moved into a shoebox-sized room that barely had enough space for them to lie down. Because there was no one else to take care of little Jaeha, his mother had to prepare the day's meals for him and leave a potty in the room before locking him up inside when she went to work. At first, he would howl at the top of his voice for her to open the door, but soon he realized how hard she was fighting back her tears whenever she stepped out. He stopped crying and learned to spend the whole day with his only friend – the TV that they'd picked up from somewhere. Jaeha was always alone, but once he turned on the TV, there were many happy faces on the screen – children his age, ajusshis and ajummas styled to the nines. Whenever he got sick of watching TV, he would pull up a chair next to the window. For hours at a time, he'd stand on the chair, staring out of the window at the passers-by until the streetlights flickered on.

Yet his mum would still not be home.

It was only after Jaeha, exhausted from waiting, fell asleep that she would quietly return with a black plastic bag filled with leftover banchan from the restaurant. Jaeha could smell her return. Grilled meat, charcoal, sweat, food stains and medicated patches. As he breathed in the smells, he'd finally relax into a deep sleep. The smells stuck to him. He quickly learned to handle household chores on his own, with the hope that he could at least help to wipe away one of her smells.

'I want to forget the memories of waiting for her, and the metal chains she locked the door with that made me tremble each time they clanged, knowing that I shouldn't cry.'

'How lonely and terrified you must have been.'

'My greatest fear was Ms Yeonja not coming home. That scared me the most. Whenever the panic consumed me, I would think back to the movies I'd watched on TV. I played the scenes in my head over and over, and imagined how the story would continue. From there, I developed an interest in making my own movies. Ha ha . . . funny, isn't it? That was how I got into filmmaking.'

'Absolutely not. There's nothing funny about this. It's sad.'

'You're right. It's sad. Actually, it's liberating to be able to admit that I'm sad. It's not easy to do that.'

Jieun paused. 'I know.'

'Sajangnim, please help Ms Yeonja. Help her forget how she used to weep whenever she locked the door behind her.'

'What about your own pain?'

'Of course, I'd love to make it go away. But now that I'm older, even though I still don't fully understand, I've come to appreciate how Ms Yeonja was trying her hardest to raise me. In those days, she was even younger than I am now. Barely twenty-nine,' said Jaeha. 'Oh wow. I sounded so cool just now, didn't I?'

'. . . Er, well. It's very admirable that you can see it that way.'

Jaeha continued to smile as always, but he couldn't hide the slight quiver at the corner of his mouth. Jieun took his t-shirt.

'I'll extend an opening day special to you. Two for one. Since you're already here, I'll remove the stain for you, and next time, you can bring Ms Yeonja and I'll help her, too.'

'Really? You'd do that?'

'Yes, anytime. Come, let's get started. Once the stain is removed, it'll be gone forever. But remember, it's possible that related memories will also be wiped away. Are you OK with that? No regrets?'

'No regrets. Even if there are, I'll live with them.'

He clenched his jaw, resolute. If possible, he'd love to get rid of it all. Memories of those days, the years spent on films, the moment he received the award – everything. He wanted to wipe the slate clean of all traces of movies and moviemaking. Deep down, what he truly wanted to erase was the pain he'd suffered in his childhood. To do that, he must also wash away the pain Ms Yeonja had endured.

After getting through yet another day, they would fall asleep holding hands, seeking warmth in each other. He often prayed for morning not to come, because when the sun rose, melancholy would creep up on Ms Yeonja. She knew she would soon have to lock the door behind her again.

Jieun waved her hand gracefully in front of the washing machine. The door swung open, and with a whoosh, Jaeha's stained t-shirt was sucked in.

One, two, three, four, five, six, seven.

Tears pooled in Jaeha's eyes as he counted the spins. *Goodbye, loneliness. Goodbye, little Jaeha. Goodbye, my love for movies.*

'Do you know what's most important in life?' Jieun asked a few moments later as they stood shoulder to shoulder watching the washing machine.

Jaeha looked sideways at Jieun but didn't reply. Unperturbed, she continued.

'To breathe. Breathing is the single most important thing in life. We need to breathe properly to live well. Don't you think so?'

'I didn't expect you to say that.'

'Well, if you aren't breathing, how do you expect to live? Breathe well, live well. Breathe, eat and work. Take in the disappointments and revel in the happy moments. Say what's on your mind, hate and love to your heart's content. Working, sleeping, walking and breathing. That's what life is all about. But before you can sleep soundly, eat well and laugh from your heart, first, you need to be breathing.'

'Hmm, breathing . . .'

'Yes, only when our breathing is relaxed will we have the strength to face our problems head-on and live each day as it comes. There's no such thing as a life of smooth sailing. All we can do is try to prevail over issues as they arise. Avoidance doesn't solve a problem – you need to face it and work through it. That's what it means to overcome.'

'But if it means we can't hide from or escape anything, isn't that too harsh?'

'It's tough, of course. But once we've lived through the difficult times, the problem will stop being an issue. It's the same with the blemishes on our heart. Once we acknowledge their presence, they're no longer stains but growth rings.

'Don't be afraid of life. No one knows for sure whether we'll live to see a certain day, so why think too far ahead about an unformed future? Don't fret over what lies ahead. Be present in the moment and when tomorrow comes, it'll be a brand-new day – yet another *today.* That's good enough.'

'How do you know so much about life? You must be at most a couple of years older than me. Yet you speak like you've lived a thousand years.'

A smile tugged at the corner of Jieun's mouth. *Child, you're smart. Though, actually, it's been more than a thousand years.*

The washing machine rattled to a stop and the door clicked open. A whirlwind of red petals, identical to the ones that had conjured up the building, danced in welcome. In moments, they had rearranged themselves into a beam of red light that carried the t-shirt back to Jaeha. He hesitated for a moment. The largest of the stains had vanished, and the remaining patches were a shade lighter. A couple of petals turned cartwheels around his wrists, as if urging him to take the shirt.

'Go up to the rooftop and hang it on the laundry line. It'll dry in the sun tomorrow and the stain will disappear forever.'

Jaeha accepted his shirt. For a minute, he stood perfectly still, a little stunned, a little at a loss for words. He wasn't sad at all. He was always sad, but not today. Had this mysterious laundry helped him erase the stain on his heart? He wiped the smile off his face – the smile he used to mask his sadness – and with a neutral expression, he headed to the rooftop garden.

'What a strange place. The owner, too,' Jaeha muttered.

He called out to Jieun, who was about to head downstairs.

'Sajangnim, why here? Why Marigold? Of all places, why did your mind laundry come to bloom here?'

'. . . Marigolds were my mother's favourite flower. And because of the sunsets. They're gorgeous.'

'Aren't there many other places with breathtaking sunsets?'

'Sure. But they don't have a snack shop next door that serves delicious kimbap.'

'Huh? The kimbap? Wow, you have terrible taste. I'll take you somewhere else next time. You need an introduction to the Jaechelin Guide – I know the best places.'

'All right, someday,' said Jieun before heading downstairs.

Behind her, Jaeha was still shaking his head.

Jieun thought back to the sunset that day, the day she first woke up in Marigold. Today's was just as gorgeous.

Chapter IV

YEONHEE

'Help me get rid of the stain left by love.'

As Jieun came downstairs, Yeonhee closed her book with trembling hands. In her job at the department store beauty section, she had met so many different types of people that she had learned to suss out their personalities at a single glance. With nothing to do while waiting for customers to turn up at her tiny little counter, she'd got into the habit of reading people as they passed.

When Jaeha, who was usually so deeply suspicious, had followed Jieun upstairs to the first floor, Yeonhee could feel the air in the room lighten. The easing of the atmosphere was a sign that Jieun was to be trusted. At the very least, she didn't come across as a liar. At first, Yeonhee had thought she'd walked straight into a pyramid scheme, and that Jieun was trying to lure her with strange promises, but there seemed to be nothing for sale here. Perhaps it was true that the laundry could really wash out the blemishes on the heart and mind. Or rather, she found herself wanting to believe so.

'Why would love leave a stain?' Jieun asked, patting her on the shoulder.

Yeonhee reminded her of a shivering stray cat huddled in a corner that perked up when a person approached with food.

'I knew he was seeing another girl, but I thought I'd always be his one true love,' Yeonhee opened up to her. 'He was never unfaithful to begin with. For the first three years, we were inseparable. We'd text each other all night until our phones overheated. We were each other's first loves.

'Unlike me, Heejae had big dreams. I used to love how his eyes sparkled when he spoke about them. I didn't have any goals in life. I only did what I was supposed to, and what I had to. So, when Heejae wanted to try his hand at composing songs, I bought him a decent laptop on a twenty-four-month instalment. Then he told me he wanted to perform his songs himself, so I gave him a guitar. And when he changed his mind and wanted a keyboard, I got him a keyboard. And then a mic when he wanted to sing his own songs.'

Yeonhee spoke softly and turned her head to the window.

Before long, she'd found herself paying for his living expenses when he ended up moving in with her. They had many happy shared memories, though – shopping for groceries and cooking meals at home, having long naps and heading to the park for walks in their loungewear, throwing their heads back in laughter at random things. Faded memories came bubbling to the surface, and Yeonhee fell deeper into thought.

Jieun subconsciously took a handkerchief and gripped it.

What is love? What's so special about it that it can make a person trust so wholeheartedly?

'Aren't I the fool?' said Yeonhee. 'But at that time, he was my everything. He dabbled in music composition for a while and then said he wanted vocal classes. Before long, it was acting school . . . I ended up taking on extra part-time jobs at night, working at the convenience store and waitressing in restaurants so I could support his dreams. At the time, I thought it was OK for the one with the means to earn to do so, and it wasn't like I had anything to spend it on anyway. If realizing his dreams could make Heejae happy, I thought I would be happy, too. At some point, he became my dream. Now that I think about it, perhaps I was hoping to achieve the dreams I never had through him.'

Soon after Heejae started vocal classes, he suddenly stopped texting so much. She'd believed him when he said he was too busy practising. But when he switched to acting classes, he started disappearing for nights on end. When he came home for the first time in days, he was drunk. All he did was sleep. And without bothering to speak, he would pack a change of clothes and walk out. There were even times he showed his face just once a month. Three months passed like this, then six months, a year. Their connection died out. Physically and emotionally.

'His touch – his body, his hands – felt cold and awkward. There was no more burning desire, no tenderness. I hated how our bodies were reacting mechanically to each other, so I started shunning his touch. We still lived together, but we were neither lovers nor friends.

'One Saturday afternoon, he came back home reeking of alcohol, imploring me to take out a loan. His mother had fallen ill, and her surgery would cost ten million won. He would get a job soon, he promised, and repay the money. That day, for the first time in a long while, we ate together at the dining table. He grilled mackerel and made soybean paste stew. I remember how shiny and fluffy the rice turned out. We sat opposite each other and polished off the last grain, and naturally ended up in bed for a long night together. Deeper, heavier and hotter than any other time. I believed he was sincere. The body doesn't lie.'

Finally, she had got hold of his heart again. It was bittersweet, but Yeonhee was awash with relief. *Let's start anew and return to our loving beginnings. We'll spend the rest of our lives together, like a normal family.* It was what Yeonhee yearned for – a real family who travelled through life together.

The next day, to get to the bank in time, she took half a day off from work and returned home early. When she opened the front door, she felt her breathing stop. Placed neatly next to Heejae's slippers at the entrance was a pair of heels. Heels she'd never seen before. The two pairs of shoes were arranged side by side, pointing towards the door. Size 230. Small feet. Yeonhee could hear muffled moans coming from their room. She closed her eyes. Should she scream? Take photographic evidence? Call the police? Or Jaeha . . . ? She stood stiffly for a moment before stretching out an arm, fingers trembling. She grabbed the heels, spun around and stepped back out, closing the door behind her.

'Why did I take them? I had no idea. But I hurled those

dainty heels down the stairs, and they broke. Like our relationship, the heels were so flimsy.'

Jieun fixed her deep-set eyes on Yeonhee, giving her a moment to collect herself.

Yeonhee looked up, wiping away her tears with the handkerchief Jieun handed her. She gave Jieun a small smile. *A tearful smile*, Jieun thought. A minute passed before Yeonhee spoke again.

'I thought it would take us a long time to talk about breaking up. Heejae was the conflict-avoidant type, and he didn't know how to set boundaries. He'd let anyone stay by his side, and when you left him, he wouldn't try to hold on to you. Even though I knew he had no sense of self-direction, I wanted to be the one to fill his heart.'

Not everyone could be happy in love. But the more she loved, the emptier she became. The first one to fall deep is often the one hoping for the other to rise up to meet them.

Yeonhee watched as Jieun topped up her tea. She reached for the cup, fingers embracing its warmth. She swallowed hard and continued.

'You won't know how things turn out until you see them through, so I did. I'm not the type who can simply dust off my pride and leave. And I'm no good at holding back my feelings and playing mind games, either. I really am a fool, aren't I?'

Jieun listened in silence.

'I want to wipe away all the memories of having loved Heejae. It must've been love to him at some point, or so I hoped. We shared many tender memories, and now I think of him whenever I smile, whenever I feel happy. But sadness always clouds it over.'

We cry and ache when we fall out of love. But the saddest thing is, because of the blissful memories of having loved, we can't even bring ourselves to hate that person. Life goes on, just as the memories remain.

'OK. So put on the t-shirt I gave you and concentrate on those memories. They'll bleed into the shirt.'

'How do I wash off the stains?'

'We'll decide after we've taken a look. The washing machine will work to remove some of the marks, but others may require handwashing.'

'Oh . . . OK.'

Yeonhee turned her mind back to the days of the relationship and pulled the t-shirt over her head, leaving make-up on the white collar. What a mess. *Chaos follows me wherever I go.* She was looking forward to changing into a fresh shirt after washing away her pain, but now she'd added a new stain before she'd even begun. She ran a finger over the smudge of red and in that moment, she was reminded of the lipstick stain on Heejae's collar. A shade she hadn't recognized. More memories flitted across her mind – how she'd tried to hide because she was afraid that she'd run into Heejae with another woman in his arms. Yeonhee felt her heart tighten.

'It's OK. You're hurting, that's normal. To feel the pain means you've done your best and followed your heart.'

'But these spots . . . they're so dark.'

'They're stains. That's how they look. Remember, no one in the world is pristine. Come, follow me.'

Yeonhee walked behind Jieun, pressing the increasingly spotted t-shirt close to her. She'd imagined traces of love burning into a black crisp or curling up in wispy grey smoke, so she felt oddly detached to see them as ordinary stubborn stains. She hugged the memories of love close, as if embracing Heejae, too.

I'm glad.

'What was that?' said Jieun.

'Oh, it's nothing. By the way, have you given up teleporting?'

'I have. I'm trying to get used to walking. Let's go to the room where clothes get washed by hand.'

Moving ahead of Yeonhee, Jieun's steps were light and graceful.

The wooden door beside the bar table opened into a room enclosed by white walls. Its lights cast a warm glow. Trickling through the centre of the room was a stream. The clear water seemed to murmur as it flowed gently over rocks, and occasionally a bird made a sound overhead. Yeonhee bit down a scream. Had she actually walked into a forest?

'Gosh! Where are we? How can there be a brook in the middle of a room?'

'Because we're at the mind laundry.'

'Did you cast a spell?'

'This isn't magic, it's . . . well, something. But see, isn't it gorgeous here? Looks exactly like the village I'm from.'

Was it her eyes playing tricks on her? Yeonhee thought she saw a shadow of melancholy flit across Jieun's expression even as she broke into a faint smile. Yeonhee nodded absently as she took off the white shirt.

'Will the stains be gone after I've washed it in this stream?'

'Yes. If it's a stain that can be erased, it'll grow fainter. Should you change your mind, feel free to stop anytime. It's up to you.' Jieun handed her a bar of white soap and a bucket, then left the room.

Alone, Yeonhee hesitated before holding up the shirt. What would remain once the memories were gone? Without love, what was left? She wanted to wipe away all traces of him, but there was also a voice within her whispering otherwise. How ironic.

'Forget it. Let me stop worrying and just try dipping it in the water. When will I ever get a chance to do this again?'

Yeonhee rolled back her sleeves and filled the bucket. She lowered the shirt into the water and, as it made contact, the white walls of the room began to glow. A rush of memories swept through her, unfolding in front of her eyes.

Their heart-fluttering first meeting, the day their fingertips kept brushing as they walked side by side until at last he held her hand in a silent promise; the delicious grilled pork belly which they ate on the rooftop of her rented room on her payday; the days spent glued to each other, him walking her home from work; sleeping in on her days off; fetching ice cream from the neighbourhood mart in their slippers after cooking ramyeon for lunch; the earbuds and the music they shared on the subway; the times when their hearts beat in tandem; their peals of laughter; the days spent in love, supporting each other, offering each other a shoulder to lean on; then his sighs, suffocated by her clinginess that only worsened as she spiralled deeper into loneliness; the flesh memory of her stubbornly gripping on to him, desperately hoping he hadn't already moved on.

As the images flashed past, Yeonhee saw more happiness than melancholy – the radiant smile on her face as he made her laugh.

I was glowing with love.

Deep down, Yeonhee had known that even though he hadn't asked to break up, Heejae was no longer in love with her. He was getting tired of their relationship, but she was so mired in loneliness that he was reluctant to suggest they stop seeing each other, so he started seeing someone else instead. When she suspected, she pretended she hadn't. Indeed, they were both to blame. Whether for loving each other or falling out of love, they were both responsible.

Yet she hadn't been able to accept the breakup; she'd chosen to resent him instead. For refusing to come back to her even when she missed him so badly. With hate as an excuse, she could still think of him. She couldn't bear to let such precious memories fade into nothing, so she bound them tight with resentment and kept them close to her, even though she knew it would only drain her. Her heart became increasingly battered, narrowing the space a new love could occupy. It was time now. Time to stop wearing herself down, to leave space for a love that might – no, would – come one day.

'Sorry . . . Thank you . . . I missed you. And I loved you so much.'

Yeonhee scooped out the shirt from the stream and held it close to her, as if embracing the fragments of memories. The stain had lightened considerably.

Jieun, who had come quietly back into the room, laid a hand on Yeonhee's shoulder. 'Half of the resentment has gone,' she said.

'I'll stop here. The memories of having loved . . . I want to cherish them.'

There was no one else in the room, but Yeonhee wailed like a child desperate for attention. Never before had she cried this hard. As her tears splashed into the stream, the water twinkled and suddenly vanished, turning into a whirl of crimson petals that whisked her to the rooftop.

'Nothing can shock me any more,' Yeonhee murmured. Swallowing her tears, she let herself be carried away by the flying petals.

Having caught a glimpse of the clothes lines from the lower floor, she walked purposefully towards them. Fluttering in the wind, the clothes from afar had looked white, but up close, she realized that many had smudges and stains of different shapes and sizes. Whose clothes were these, she wondered, as she weaved through the lines and chose an empty spot for her t-shirt.

It was time to lay down her burden. She could lean on someone in times of loneliness, but love would never fill that void inside her. The emptier her heart, the tighter she had tried to cling on to Heejae, and in turn, he distanced himself from her. By refusing to accept that he was drifting away, she – not him – was the one left hurt. In those days, she'd had no idea that love could change like the seasons. That what followed spring might not be summer, but a harsh winter.

She now understood that only after the relationship had

ended would there be any love. These memories of love wouldn't fade. Their power would linger and glow. Instead of choosing to forget, she could let those memories live on, and cherish them. On days when she felt like she'd lost her spark, she could relive the beautiful times she'd had. *I'll remember how happy I was, how I glowed, and the loving memories we shared. Surely that'll warm my empty heart?* Yeonhee was finally ready to bid Heejae goodbye. A goodbye no longer tainted by hate or resentment.

Jieun looked sideways at Yeonhee as she hung up her t-shirt, the stains lightened, but still visible. She could feel peace emanating from her. The kind of relief that comes over you when you put down a weight.

'I've been around for much longer than you can imagine, so I could give you some words of advice, but I won't do that. Instead, I'll give you a present.'

'You look younger than me, though?'

'Yeah, I've been told I have a baby face. Here, wear this.'

Jieun handed her a t-shirt with a heart-shaped smudge above the chest.

'What a pretty print.'

Yeonhee stared at it for a moment before putting it on on top of her clothes. She sniffed at it, taking in the smell of sunshine. She felt strength well up in her. *That's right. We're all standing tall like trees.* From now on, she'd no longer lean on anyone. She'd learn to stand strong on her own. This was the first time she had ever had the courage to do so.

'When I soaked the t-shirt, the memories came rushing back to me. I realized how happy I'd been in love. But it occurred to me how much I am smiling because now I love myself, not someone else. I don't want to erase those stains. If I happen to think back to those painful memories, I'll allow myself to feel the pain. Same goes for the happy times. I'll love myself more, more than anyone else will.'

Yeonhee's voice was trembling.

'Just smile,' said Jieun. 'Smile like you're happy.'

'Even when I'm not?'

'Yes. The human brain is naive. It can't distinguish between real and imaginary happiness. As long as you smile, your brain will process that as happiness. It's like playing a trick on your mind.'

'Huh?'

'Try it. Once the brain believes that you're happy, it'll naturally get you to smile. And a smile attracts people with positive energy.'

Using two of her fingers, Jieun pulled the corners of her lips upwards into a smile. Yeonhee did the same. At the sight of their mouths curving up into a smile that didn't quite reach their eyes, they both burst out laughing.

'Hey, you yourself don't actually know how to smile, do you?' Yeonhee teased.

'Of course I do. If not, would I be telling you what to do?'

They glanced at each other and giggled. It was the first time in a while that Jieun had laughed. So this was how it felt. *Definitely worth playing a trick for*, she thought.

'To tell you the truth, I've decided that from today onwards, I will smile, too. While I can't dictate where life takes me, at least I can choose whether to smile or cry.'

'Woah, look at my goosebumps!' Yeonhee said. 'You mean even *you* can't decide where life is heading?'

Jieun's face slowly fell.

'If I had the choice, I wouldn't be here right now. Come on, the night wind is chilly. Let's head downstairs.'

From behind, Jieun looked so forlorn that Yeonhee had the urge to hug her.

She had a thought and pulled out a pen from her pocket. She took off the t-shirt and wrote on it.

Dance,
Like nobody is watching you.
Love,
Like you've never been hurt.
Sing,
Like nobody is listening to you.
Work,
Like you don't need the money.
Live,
Like today is your last day to live.
Alfred D. Souza

Yeonhee pulled the cleaned t-shirt back on. *What an incredible place this is.*

'Can Jaeha and I visit whenever we're free?'

'We are a laundry service, not a playground.'

'But aren't you always alone? We can come and help you. After all, we're your very first customers. We'll bring soju. Or do you prefer wine?'

'Neither. I don't drink. Come on, time to go. Don't you need to work today? The sun is rising soon.'

'It's Saturday. OK, we'll head home for today. But let's share a laugh again next time.'

It had been a long time since she'd felt such hope, the flutter in her heart that everything would turn out well. Yeonhee looked behind her and a smile spread across her face. Her heart was strangely at peace. She turned her attention towards the enigmatic owner of the mind laundry.

'Oh . . . uhm . . . Sajangnim!'

'What is it?'

'You mentioned the village where you used to live. What was it like there?'

'You and Jaeha are super-close, aren't you?'

'Yes! How did you know?'

'You both have way too many questions. Stop talking nonsense and scoot home. I'm tired.'

This time, Jieun was the one who turned to stare out of the window. Arms folded, she closed her eyes, looking as though she might fall asleep on her feet. Not wanting to disturb her, Yeonhee and Jaeha quietly slipped away.

Chapter V

EUNBYUL

'Miss, are you awake? Blink if you can hear me.'

Eunbyul stirred at the noise. She blinked, twice, her long lashes fluttering closed before opening again. Each second seemed to stretch on. She closed her eyes. Her breathing was even, as if she were in a deep slumber. Two nurses who'd just entered the ward stole a glance at her face and whispered to each other.

'That woman lying there, is she a celebrity? I'm sure I've seen her somewhere else.'

'Yeah, probably online. She's a . . . What do you call them? *In-flu*-something. You know, like a celebrity, with a huge Instagram following.'

'Ahh, an influencer! Does she have a lot of followers?'

'The last I saw, probably a million? Let's check.'

'Never mind, don't bother. But why did she overdose on sleeping pills again?'

'Who knows. If I were her, I'd be thanking the gods and living my life to the fullest. Wasn't she brought in just a couple of months ago?'

'Yeah. I've seen her here twice, or is it the third time? And she's so young. Tsk-tsk.'

'Remember how her whole family flocked to the ward that time? What a commotion – all that wailing and weeping.'

'Ah – is she the one who sold those cosmetics on her Instagram? Which got busted for containing harmful ingredients? It was all over the news.'

'Oh yeah. Did something terrible happen?'

'She claimed the products were made of all-natural ingredients, but they weren't. Many people complained they got skin problems after using them. That got her a ton of hate comments. There were even people who created anti-fan accounts just to bash her.'

The other nurse tutted. 'She's only twenty-three but already scamming people with her shoddy products?'

'You think she even made them herself? She probably sourced them from somewhere and was raking in the commission fees. I remember when it all blew up, they reported that she posted an apology saying that she'd refund the customers out of her own pocket and even went to volunteer at an animal shelter. Yeah, I'm going to follow her on Instagram. I want her life. Anyway, we'd better go – there's a nurse call.'

'OK. Hey, since she's asleep, shall we sneak a photo and post it online?'

'Shh! Have you forgotten what happened to that intern?

Saddled with a lawsuit on top of a disciplinary hearing at the hospital. Let's go before she wakes up.'

'OK. But wow, she's so pretty even when asleep. I'd love to look like *that*!'

The two nurses left the ward. The moment Eunbyul heard the door slide to a close, she opened her eyes.

Not again.

How tiresome.

So she'd failed this time, too. Just how many sleeping pills must she actually take to never wake up again? She blinked several times before closing her eyes. By now, the media must have caught wind of the news. It was probably a frenzy outside. *Enough is enough.* Eunbyul pulled the blanket over her head.

I want to end my miserable life.

'A celeb influencer with a strong 1.9-million following on Instagram' was how the media described Eunbyul, who had debuted as a model in her teens. Early in her career, she'd gone on an extreme water-only diet and lost ten kilograms in a month, along with her health. After that health scare, she'd started to exercise, eat proper meals and read voraciously, and when she shared her healing journey on Instagram, she shot to instant fame as an icon for teenage girls and women in their twenties. Stylish, charismatic and eloquent, she basically went viral overnight. Eunbyul's life, her every move, took the internet by storm.

At first, Eunbyul basked in her newfound fame and the slew of advertisement love-calls. To make even more money and get more likes, she began to painstakingly curate her online content, posting stuff that she knew would go viral. Sponsorship deals came knocking on her door – branded clothes, bags, shoes, luxury services, even imported cars. Often, she'd be invited by well-known brands to attend fashion shows. Her posts always generated buzz. Journalists loved her as they knew her articles were guaranteed hits. As time passed, her life inside those Instagram squares grew increasingly luxurious.

However, off the grid, Eunbyul didn't have a single confidante. Because she'd quit high school midway through to start modelling, she barely got to meet potential friends her age. Once she became a celebrity, she was always surrounded by older adults at work. She might be living the high life, but alone, her smile faded by the day. There were things she gained – wealth and fame – but the brighter she shone, the deeper her loneliness grew. On days she didn't have to work, she'd weep in her darkened room. Even then, she reassured herself that she'd be fine. After all, she still had her family.

My family is all that's left. But that's enough.

Eunbyul was the oldest of the three siblings. When her career took off, she used her earnings to move her family from a two-room flat to a fifty-pyeong luxury apartment in the glitzy Gangnam district. She didn't come from a well-to-do family. When she was young, she didn't even dare to tell her parents how much she craved fried chicken for fear of adding to their burden. Instead, she silently resolved to earn lots of money so that her parents could stop fighting, and she would no longer have to tiptoe around them or shield her siblings' ears from their screaming matches. She was convinced that if she could earn enough to break free of the life of monthly rentals, their lives would improve. Surely having money would make her family happier? And yet . . .

'Eunbyul-ah, Mummy wants that department store V-I . . . You know, the thing they give to the rich ajummas who spend a lot so they can join this exclusive group that meets for coffee in the afternoons? What do you call that VIP card? Something about jasmine black . . . Whatever that is, I want it, too. Raise my card limit for me.'

'Daddy has a new business idea . . .'

'Noona, I'm going to be a YouTuber. Can you buy me the camera and gear and appear in my videos for now?'

'Eonnie, Gucci just released their newest collection and I've been eyeing that bag. I'll go ahead and get it, OK?'

With her family, it was always about money. In the past when they used to be able to afford only one fried chicken for all of them, everyone was happy to give up their share to one another. How did it come to this . . . ? These days, if she were to show the slightest hesitation because the demands were beyond her means, they'd band together and make it seem as though she was the unfeeling one.

Because she was afraid to lose them – the people closest to her in the world – Eunbyul could only find more ways to earn the money to satisfy their wants. A few months ago, she'd started selling products on her Instagram, bringing in brands spanning fashion, diet supplements, cosmetics and even household appliances. Believing whatever the companies told her, she actively promoted an 'all-natural' make-up brand. Of course, her followers trusted her and bought whatever she recommended.

It was morning again. Even without an alarm clock, her eyes automatically opened at exactly the same time. She had got rid of the clock when she read somewhere that a quiet environment would help her sleep better, and for good measure, she kept the furniture in her bedroom to a bare minimum. Not that her insomnia had ever got any better.

'Shit . . . my head hurts. Where's my phone?'

Her typical morning routine was always to spend her first waking moments on the emotional rollercoaster of social media metrics, as though the numbers were charting her lifeline. But her sleeping pills always gave her a splitting headache the next morning. Ever since she'd first started modelling, she'd been taking medication for insomnia. She liked how the pills made her fall asleep within fifteen minutes, so she took them regularly. Soon, one pill was no longer enough, but whenever she asked to replenish her supplies, the doctor would warn her about the side effects. She'd ignore the advice, and took to switching hospitals each time to stock up. Better sleeping pills than alcohol, right? She needed to sleep to function at work. Only then could she take more photos and earn more money. But with a perpetual buzz in her ears – like an annoying mosquito – sleep continued to evade her. And there was the problem of the throbbing headaches.

'What should I post today?'

Even though her body felt heavy and she could barely open

her eyes, she extended an arm towards her bedside table and felt around until she found her phone. She pushed up her sleep mask, squinting at the screen as she opened Instagram. Her eyes zeroed in on the follower count before checking the number of likes and comments.

'What? Only 30,000 likes for yesterday's post? Hmm . . . I wonder what the problem is. A sponsored post shouldn't get so little engagement. What a disaster!' She chewed her fingernails anxiously.

But it was even worse than it seemed. As she scrolled, all she could see was complaints rolling in – skin rashes, bleeding, itching, inflammation and more.

Over the day, the number of anti-fans swelled, and she was slapped with several lawsuits. It turned out the make-up lacked proper testing and certification.

Eunbyul was scared.

She called her mother.

'Mum . . . I . . .'

'I'm at the golf club now. Have you taken care of the card limit for me? I'm supposed to buy the others a meal later.'

'Mum, it's not the time to be treating people to lunches. I . . .'

'Can't speak now, got to go. It's my turn! Don't forget about the card limit!'

Eunbyul sighed, then called her dad. She'd never got into such a mess before, and it was frightening. The hate comments were breaking through the floodgates, inundating not just her social media but also her news articles. The owner of the cosmetics brand who had sweetened the deal by offering her 30 per cent commission was now uncontactable. She trembled. It felt as though the whole world was criticizing and hating on her.

'Dad . . . I . . .'

Her dad, who finally picked up on the fifth call, yelled at her the moment the call connected.

'The internet is exploding! What the hell is going on?'

'It's because . . .'

'I'm launching my health food business today but look at what the news articles are saying! Post up an apology on your page right now! Say you're sorry!'

Eunbyul cut the call. She had to think. First, she had to put up an apology post. And settle the refunds . . . What next? After sending a text to her lawyer, she scrolled through the never-ending notifications on her phone. Biting her lip in resolve, she turned off her phone. If only she could disappear, too. Eunbyul shrugged out of the branded outfit that hung on her paper-thin frame, changed into a pair of white poplin pyjamas, and slowly walked towards her vanity table. Pulling open the drawer, she reached deep inside for her bottle of sleeping pills.

Let this misery end. Please.

'Urgh . . . my head. Where am I? What am I doing in the car?'

Eunbyul coughed as she woke with a splitting headache. She reached for the bottled water by the driver's seat and took several large gulps to soothe her parched throat. Her senses began to sharpen up. She adjusted her car seat back to an upright position, looked around and stumbled out of the car. How far had she actually driven?

She remembered waking up at the hospital but had no recollection of driving anywhere. She must have been hallucinating or sleepwalking – likely side effects from the sleeping pills. Hunching down, she looked at herself in the side mirror. She was wearing a full face of make-up and a white tweed suit. She straightened, checking herself in the window. Her hair was nicely styled, as if she had been about to attend a fashion show after a visit to the hair salon. But what was she doing in this strange neighbourhood?

Her head continued to throb. It was a familiar pain but still, she couldn't get used to it. Would she ever be numb to misery and pain, or could she release herself from their grip? She threaded her fingers through her hair and took in her surroundings.

'Oh my god! What a charming village, with the sea there, and a city on the other side. A seaside city! How cool is that!'

She marvelled at the landscape. It had been a while since she'd last visited anywhere new. When was the last time she'd had the opportunity to enjoy the ocean? The wind caressed her cheeks, and she closed her eyes. So relaxing. She spread her arms wide. Something seemed to stir within her. A sense of deja vu in this unfamiliar place. The sky was covered by a thick blanket of fog, but even so, it felt oddly calming. She inhaled deeply. The moist air filling her lungs felt good.

'Mmm, the salty air . . . I feel so alive.'

She started to walk but when she almost tripped on a rock, she decided not to venture out further. Relieving her feet of her nine-centimetre heels, she headed back to her car barefoot, feeling the ache in her calves as her shoes dangled from her hands. She opened the car boot and tossed them in, taking out a pair of sneakers wedged between the shoeboxes. She liked to match her footwear with her clothes, so she always had several pairs in her car.

What a picture-perfect neighbourhood! Feels like I've travelled to the edge of the world. An image of a village next to the sea taken from the top of a hill? Photos would surely go viral. Mmm, maybe I should do a travel series . . . Oh shit. Where's the phone charger? Shit! I can't miss any important calls or messages. Damn this headache . . .

She needed to charge her phone. And if she was going to shoot some photos, she'd better get a change of clothes. Would there be any decent shops around? At the very least, she'd need a new jacket so it wouldn't be obvious that all the photos were taken on the same day. Her mind was abuzz. If she didn't post for a day, she might become irrelevant. What if her follower count dropped? Anxiety and obsession had become her constant companions, edging out any pleasure and peace in her life. She knew she wasn't happy, but at least within the squares, she wanted to be her best self.

At least I'm happy somewhere. Whenever the darkness threatened to engulf her, she'd comfort herself. It was all she could do to stop herself from going over the edge. Away from the lens, she was in the shadows. As if when the camera was off, she'd switch off too. And once the camera started rolling, she'd come back to life. She wanted to know what was wrong with her, yet she was afraid of the answer. If she continued like this, wouldn't it all end someday? Anyway, it was time to get to work.

'OK, I need to do a live. Get a change of clothes. Find a scenic café. Maybe I should stroll around a bit. Actually, a good coffee now – an iced americano – would hit the spot. Maybe an extra shot for the oomph. Mmm, let's see.'

She was alone most of the time, so Eunbyul was used to talking to herself. She set off to explore the neighbourhood. Small houses dotted the stretch of road – it was a modest village. Oddly, she was enveloped by a sense of belonging and ease as she walked down the street, admiring the rows of little flowerpots. Would there be a café nearby?

In the distance, she spotted a woman in a gorgeous dress printed with red flowers, her jet-black hair tied up neatly. *She looks like a good person to ask*. Their eyes met.

'Excuse me. Is there a café or clothes store nearby?'

'A café? Nope. You'll have to head to the entrance of the village. Are you new here?'

'Oh, yeah. I'm kind of lost . . . I need a change of clothes and a place to do an Insta live.'

'A live?'

'Yeah . . . Don't you know who I am?'

'Hmm . . . afraid not. Who are you?'

'Ah, never mind. I guess you're not on Instagram. Ha ha. But you might have seen me in ads.'

As someone who was used to being recognized in the street, Eunbyul was surprised by the woman's reaction. *How doesn't she know me? Or is she pretending not to?* Eunbyul pursed her small, pretty lips.

Jieun read her thoughts. 'Uhm, I have no idea what Insta is; I don't have it. I listen to the radio. Don't even watch TV.'

'Whoa! There are still people listening to the radio? Do you really not know who I am?'

'I don't. But I'll get to know you starting now. Your name is?'

'Eunbyul. If you search it up, you'll see it immediately.'

'OK. I'll do that. Anyway, if you need a change of clothes, I run a laundry service. It's not a clothes store, but perhaps I can lend you something?'

'For real? That'd be awesome.'

'I'll make sure to wash them clean and have them sent back to you.'

'Can you also iron out the creases on my skirt?'

'Sure. Perfect timing, since I'm on my way to work. Follow me.'

'OK, Eonnie! Can I call you that – big sister? I'm twenty-three, so you should be older than me, right?'

Eunbyul slipped her arm into Jieun's and chattered away. The moment their eyes met, Eunbyul had felt an overwhelming urge to share everything. Was it because she hadn't had a chance to confide in anyone in a long time? Or had she been sucked into that pair of deep-set eyes? Somehow this stranger had completely disarmed her, laying bare her every emotion.

It was dawn when Jieun had first spotted Eunbyul's car. She'd been about to lock up and head home when the red sports car had screeched to a halt close by. The blinding headlights made her brows furrow. *How inconsiderate. At this hour!* Jieun stared over at the car. Behind the wheel sat a woman who appeared to be spacing out, allowing her tears to flow freely down her cheeks. The look in her eyes screamed, *I have no will to live.* Jieun knew that look. She considered sending the petals over to the woman to invite her into the mind laundry, but in the end she decided to wait for the moment the woman stirred from her reverie.

A few hours later, when Eunbyul finally stepped out of the car, Jieun deliberately walked slowly past her. The young woman reminded Jieun of a lost and injured hatchling. The first thing she asked for was directions to a café and a clothes store. Jieun thought she must surely need to eat. Shouldn't she be looking for a convenience store or a restaurant instead? In fact, wasn't she at all curious about where she was right now? But to this child, what mattered most was neither food nor directions, but survival. Jieun could sense this hatchling was trying her best to flap her wings, even though she was empty on the inside.

In life, there are encounters that aren't coincidence, but fate. We meet the people we're meant to meet and go where we're meant to go. *This child is fated to meet me, and that's why she's here.* From the moment Jieun had seen the shiny red car, she'd known that its driver would be her third visitor at the Marigold Mind Laundry.

'Have you eaten?' Jieun asked.

'Not yet, but I'm fine! I'm on a one-meal-a-day diet. I have to maintain a size XS to fit into my clothes.'

'I'm not a big eater either, but I'm hungry today. How about getting some kimbap with me later? There's a snack shop next door and they have kimbap. Uh . . . it's, er . . . not bad.'

Jieun finished lamely, startled by her own initiative. She usually avoided eating with others because chatting over meals felt overly intimate, as if you were sharing food and life stories at the same time. Had she really just casually invited Eunbyul to eat with her?

'Do they sell tteokbokki as well? I've been craving it!'

'Oh, so that's your favourite. Yup, they do.'

'Really? I absolutely love tteokbokki. Eonnie, do you prefer flour or rice tteok? I like both. When you're a true-blue tteokbokki lover, you won't nit-pick. But my mum always refused to let me eat it because she was afraid I'd gain weight. It's my all-time favourite food.'

The thought of having tteokbokki was making Eunbyul more excitable than usual. Eyes rounded in anticipation, she tagged behind Jieun. Who cared whether it was flour or rice? Every tteokbokki was a good tteokbokki. Maybe she should also get some soondae to dip into the spicy red sauce. Oh, not to forget the kimbap. Would they also have fritters? Perfect, just perfect. While Eunbyul had been chattering excitedly, they'd walked all the way to the laundry.

'Oh my god! Eonnie, this is a laundry? Looks like a café at the edge of the world! The ones in Ireland look exactly like this! I've seen photos! What are those flowers blooming at the door?'

'Trumpet creepers. They usually only flower in summer but I tried to get them to bloom today for a different look. Usually, we have red camellias here.'

'But isn't it autumn right now?'

'It is, but they're able to flower at the laundry. Tell you more next time.'

'Eonnie, you're amazing,' Eunbyul gushed.

All that was left was to charge her phone and she'd be ready to go live in this cosy and beautiful space. The two-storey building, sitting at the highest point of the village, with its view over the city and shrouded in fog, exuded mystery. She took in the delightful door adorned with hanging creepers and flowers in full bloom, the cosy lights and the breathtaking view outside. Her eyes sparkled in excitement. It was as if she were a high schooler again, with no worries in the world. Just yesterday she'd been wallowing in misery having failed to die, but today, she was seeing a side of herself that she hadn't seen in ages. She wondered if she deserved to be so happy, to feel such anticipation.

What a peculiar day. The woman walking around her barely had any make-up on. Why was she oozing so much charisma and mystique? Eunbyul wanted to learn her secret.

'Eonnie! What a gorgeous place. A laundry can't get more beautiful than this!'

'Indeed. Sit wherever you like or feel free to look around.'

'I love it here so much! Wait, I'd better announce my live on Stories. Eonnie, do you have a phone charger? And I forgot my cable.'

'Just pass me your phone. We don't have coffee here, only tea. I'll brew us a cup, is that all right?'

Eunbyul put her palms together in appreciation and turned to look around, her eyes brimming with curiosity. Natural light filtered through the windows, making the space feel snug. She took a deep breath. The scent of fresh laundry stirred up warm, fuzzy memories. Her mum had smelled like this too when she used to wrap Eunbyul in her arms. Wait. *Where exactly is this place*? She had forgotten to ask.

Creak.

The huge wooden door at the entrance swung open and a man walked in. He nodded to Eunbyul in greeting before calling out to Jieun.

'Sajangnim! How about having a glass of wine with us after work today?'

'Oh, it's you, Jaeha. I thought I told Yeonhee that I don't drink?'

'Why are you turning down the good stuff? Life is much more enjoyable when you're slightly tipsy. Fine, we'll start with canned beer. Beer, soju, wine, then whiskey – we'll go down the list and find something you like. How about that?'

'What's with all the alcohol all of a sudden? . . . Hey, wait. You're quitting the advertising agency?'

'Did you just use magic? How could you have known that I'm going for a job interview today? I've been applying to companies that are hiring permanent staff. I'm also going to make full use of my degree! I'm sick and tired of all the whispering behind my back. I'm going to stay in advertising!'

'Why does it matter if you do something related to your degree or not? It's your life so you should do what you want with it. Do whatever you want, Jaeha. You'll be fine.'

'Wow, I tried to throw in some lies but you caught them all! Come on, tell me. Were you reading my mind?'

Jieun chuckled. 'So what if you go from filmmaking to an advertising agency, and then leave for a permanent offer elsewhere? Who can say anything? Even if they did, who cares? It's your life. And Jaeha, if the new place is not a good fit, you can always make the switch back. Don't be hung up on what others think. Do what you want. If you feel that's the right answer, then it is. It doesn't matter how others may judge you. It's fine. People have less interest in you than you'd think.'

'*People have less interest in you than you'd think* . . . That cuts deep . . . I wanted to share that I finally got my sommelier certification, and earlier this week I passed the initial screening at a wine company that's hiring. How did you know? I did ask myself, what's a soju-drinking bloke doing dabbling in wine? But there was this time I went to a wine-tasting event because a friend didn't want to waste his ticket, and it turned out to be a talk by our country's number one wine sommelier. He had a full head of white hair – probably in his mid-seventies. He told us how he grew up in poverty and started out as a hotel bellboy before getting a job as a restaurant server and then finally becoming a sommelier. The look in his eyes – it gave me goosebumps. I found myself thinking, "I want to grow up to be like him, to age with grace, to have such a strong and unwavering gaze. I want to walk his path." That was how I got into this field . . . And it's been even more interesting than I thought. There's so much to learn.'

As she listened to Jaeha's monologue, the corners of Jieun's mouth lifted. She flashed Eunbyul a smile and went towards him – he had not moved from the door. If she didn't send him on his way, he'd probably stand there chattering the whole day. Jieun pushed open the door and rapped on it twice – *time to go*.

'Sounds good. Drop by later with Yeonhee. Even if I'm not drinking, I can provide the cups. Teacups are fine, right?'

'*What!* No, I'll bring wine glasses. See you later! You won't mind if I ask another friend, Hae-in, to join us, right? Have a good lunch at the snack shop with your new visitor. I'll be on my way to the interview. See you in the evening!'

In a neat suit and a new pair of leather shoes, Jaeha looked different from his usual self, and uncharacteristically jittery. In his hands was a document folder from the wine company – the introductory materials he'd received at his first interview. He'd brought them along for the second interview today, clutching them as though they were the most precious thing he owned.

Hearing their banter made Eunbyul smile. What a mysterious place. From the moment she stepped inside, she'd been in a good mood. Eunbyul was reminded of the saying: you smile when you're with people who smile, and cry around people who cry. Was it because it was a laundry? Eunbyul found herself strangely at ease.

This must be a neighbourhood full of lovely people.

Had her phone finished charging? She needed to do her livestream before it got dark. Perhaps she should go back and grab the fast-charge cable from her car.

'Have some tea. It's almost done. Just a few moments more.'

'Eonnie, can you really read minds? How did you know what I was thinking? O-M-G!' Eunbyul exclaimed. 'It feels like everyone in the neighbourhood knows each other.'

Eunbyul took the offered tea. It was just the right warmth, not scalding on the tongue. Her eyes rounded in surprise. It was actually delicious. Jieun watched as Eunbyul drained her cup, then passed her a white t-shirt before taking the seat opposite her at the bar table.

'This isn't just any laundry service,' Jieun said. 'We're a mind laundry. What we wash and iron are the stains on your heart, the creases within you. Eunbyul, if there's anything hurting or upsetting you, I can help.'

'A . . . mind laundry? There's such a thing?'

'Yes, right here. One of a kind. Destiny brought you here, so there must be a reason. I'm Jieun and my work is to gently cleanse away the pain in people's hearts, to offer comfort and help them heal.'

Seeing how Eunbyul was staring wide-eyed at her, Jieun was gentler and more detailed than usual in introducing herself.

She knew it took courage to speak honestly about personal pain, and to say *I want to get better*. That most people chose to bottle up their feelings, not knowing that the wounds would fester in their hearts, that they would suffer. So many went about their lives unaware that if only the biggest pains in them were soothed, then life would be so much better. Over her lifetimes, Jieun had served healing tea to many wounded souls. Right now, she could tell that the child trembling in front of her needed help.

'The choice is yours. If something is hurting you inside, put on the t-shirt, close your eyes, and slowly recall those moments. The pain will manifest as a stain, or perhaps a crease. If you want to do something about it, come upstairs and pass the t-shirt to me. If not, you could leave it here, or take it home. You decide.'

Mouth agape, Eunbyul took the t-shirt. She stared at it in silence and when she looked up, Jieun was already halfway up the stairs. Eunbyul put on the t-shirt.

What's going on? Can that eonnie really read minds?

What a bizarre day. An unfamiliar place, everything seeming out-of-the-ordinary. Was she dreaming? Perhaps. On a day shrouded by fog such as this one, even the extraordinary felt possible. The strangest thing was how she felt right now: she had an ardent desire to live.

I want to live.

I want to wash away all my pain,

and live.

'But Eonnie, if I erase that one thing, my life will be completely different. It's what I want . . . because I'm struggling so badly. Yet I'm scared to start from scratch. What will I do if people can't relate to me or stop liking me once I'm no longer famous? My family don't know how to earn their own keep. How will they survive?'

Wearing the t-shirt as a crop tee tied on one side, Eunbyul slumped down into the chair behind Jieun, who was standing by the window. *What a charismatic child,* Jieun thought. *As clear as water. Trusting, honest and pure. People can't help but lower their guard when talking to her.* It was clear to Jieun that Eunbyul was affectionate, a people person. Even when she'd learned this was a *mind* laundry, not once did Eunbyul seem at all wary, nor did she demand answers. Instead, she trusted Jieun's words and fretted over her stains.

Jieun was usually mindful not to nudge her visitors into a decision. But rules were meant to be broken. Or else she could create new rules. Now that she seemed to be on her last life, she was determined to live according to her heart. Why, though, was she so concerned about this child? Perhaps she'd met her somewhere, though her memories were all a blur.

'Don't seek understanding from someone who doesn't know you well. Do you even understand yourself? I don't understand myself.'

'You don't? But you seem like you know everything.'

'You can't judge everything by appearances. You're only seeing the side of me that I want to show, how I hope others will see me. You said you have followers. Are you close to them?'

'Not at all. I barely know any of them. I used to love hanging out with friends, but once I started modelling I had to quit school and, over time, I lost contact with everyone. The people I meet up with these days aren't exactly friends . . . More like strategic acquaintances. At some point, I started feeling so lonely.'

'It must've been hard on you. Always being subject to scrutiny yet feeling so alone. Are you OK?' Jieun spoke softly.

'It's all so overwhelming . . . Honestly . . . Really, really hard, Eonnie!'

Jieun's question had opened the floodgates and tears were streaming down Eunbyul's face. *Life is so tough.* How she wished she could let go of it all. She yearned for true friends. Friends she could send spontaneous photos to without caring how she looked, friends with whom she could be her rawest, truest self, sharing her deepest pain and struggles. Those were the kinds of friends she wanted.

Jieun was relieved. *Great. Let loose. Cry when you're sad.* She was glad to see Eunbyul letting out her pent-up feelings.

'It's OK to cry until you feel better. Nobody will come in here. Don't worry.'

'Eonnie . . . I'm struggling so badly. I want to wipe away my life as an influencer. My life is one huge stain.'

As Eunbyul sobbed, a dark spot bled on to the shirt, and the once-smooth fabric crumpled. Creases and stains can be ironed and washed away. But it takes a good cry to release the misery and pain.

'Do you cry when you're upset?'

'No . . .'

'How about showing when you're angry?'

'But how and . . . to whom?'

'To those who made you upset, of course! Cry when you're sad, vent when you're angry and smile when you're happy. That's what life is about. And if you're bored, let it show on your face. Got it?'

'Eonnie, my photo gets taken all the time. If I frown, it might end up going viral and I'm afraid what kind of articles . . .'

Eunbyul's sobs began to subside.

'Who cares if people post photos of you? So what if there are a couple of articles criticizing you? It's OK. Nobody can be perfect. That's not human.'

'Is it OK to make mistakes? Really?'

'Of course. All of us slip up at times. Apologize if it's your fault, and when someone else makes a mistake, accept their apology and be understanding. If you can't forgive them, then just accept that whatever's happened is already in the past. Life can't be easy all the time. We lose our way, go through rough patches, stumble and fail. But we dust ourselves off and get up.'

Jieun patted her shoulder. Eunbyul reached for Jieun's hands and gradually her sobs quieted. With a firm but warm gaze, Jieun continued,

'Don't bother about what others think. Prioritize yourself. When things get tough, go somewhere nice, treat yourself to a holiday. If you're angry, don't hold it in. Eat something delicious to de-stress. Learn to live for yourself, not for anyone else. Life is more beautiful than you think. Life's worth living.'

'Life's worth living?' Eunbyul murmured. 'Honestly, Eonnie, I don't want to live any more.'

'That's a valid feeling. There have been so many moments when I was sick of living, too. But even so, you'll live. Out of nowhere, something trivial will make you laugh. And life will seem liveable again. Isn't that amazing?'

'And because we're living . . . we laugh? Will there ever come a day I'll want to keep on living?'

'Hmm, you'll know. Also, no relationship is worth protecting to the extent that you lose yourself. Even if they're family or the love of your life.'

Eunbyul nodded. She took off the t-shirt and handed it solemnly to Jieun.

'Watch this. I'll show you the most beautiful thing you've ever seen.'

Jieun closed her right hand into a fist and when her fingers spread open again, crimson petals spiralled out. The tips flickered like fireflies as they carried the stained shirt into the washing machine. Round and round the machine drum spun. Her sadness lay forgotten as Eunbyul stared in fascination at the petals; and through the door, a bright light shone like the sun.

'This is my favourite moment – watching a stained shirt spinning round and round in the washing machine. Sometimes the pain turns into light, and other times, it transforms into a gathering of beautiful flowers. Not always, though.'

Hot, silent tears flowed down Eunbyul's cheeks. She'd prayed that her life as an influencer – the happiness, the sadness – would bleed into the shirt. The dazzling moments as well as the lonely ones. All along, the person trapping her inside this image had been herself. She'd been wearing ill-fitting shoes for so long, she'd forgotten that shoes shouldn't hurt in the first place.

'Eunbyul, even with all traces removed, there's no guarantee that you'll never find fame again. You may end up in the limelight once more. Will you be just as miserable then? Because you only get one chance to use our service.'

'I truly don't know.'

'Of course. You wouldn't, because you're not living that moment yet. Maybe you'll be famous, maybe you won't. But if fame does come knocking again, you'll have a much better idea of how to strike a balance between the Eunbyul on screen and off it.'

'Will I?'

'Yes. If you believe so, it'll be. Take the first step to reach out to others and they'll reciprocate. Want a tip on making true friends?'

'Yes, please!'

'The other celebrities you meet are probably just as lonely. Put down the camera and talk to them. If you want to get close to them, you'll have to take the first step and open up to them. Just as you're doing now. Be honest, and sincere.'

'But I'm scared of being rejected.'

'What's there to fear? They may appear standoffish because they're dealing with their own issues. Friendship is built with time and effort. Spend more time with them, be real, and put in your best effort. If you're simply waiting for someone to come to you, that's unrealistic, not to mention self-indulgent. Find the courage to meet people beyond the screen. For your own sake.'

A sense of calm had settled in the air. A gentle breeze blew by, carrying with it the floral scent of a warm spring, perhaps the lingering trail of the petals that had come out to greet them.

'Eonnie, are we friends now?'

'Of course. We had a heart-to-heart, didn't we? If we've shared our feelings, it doesn't matter that we're only meeting for the first time. Aren't you hungry? Let's put the t-shirt out to dry and get some tteokbokki.'

'Oh yes, tteokbokki! Where should I hang this? Up there? I'll be back in a second!'

One moment she was crying, the next she was all smiles again. How could a child with such honest emotions have held them back for so long? Watching Eunbyul sprint up the stairs, Jieun felt a fresh scent of mint spread within her. It was as if she'd become a mint plant herself. Was this the first time she'd felt so rejuvenated after helping someone? Or maybe she was just hungry. These days, her appetite was huge.

Jieun chuckled to herself and dialled Our Snack Shop.

'Ajumma. Two rolls of kimbap. Tteokbokki for two, as well as soondae with offal sides. Oh yes, and a mix of fritters too. I'll be bringing a friend, so give us a generous serving!'

'Omona! Our Jieun sajangnim is coming with a friend? How lovely. Should I make you both some noodles, too?'

'Nope. You haven't forgotten what I said about not changing the menu, right? Oh, and the tteokbokki, is it made with flour or rice? Does it even matter?'

'Of course! The texture is different. We have both. You didn't know?'

'Oh . . . of course. We'll be there soon. Throw in some fish cake for free, would you?'

As Jieun finished the call, the three of them smiled to themselves. Jieun was surprised, then shrugged. Smiling keeps us alive. And when we're living, there'll always be moments when we're truly happy.

'Eonnie. Have you been hacked? What's wrong with your account? Have you reported it to the police?'

'Eunbyul, I can't use my credit card. It was declined. What happened?'

'Eunbyul, I'll need you to do a photoshoot for my new business idea.'

After that strange and beautiful day, Eunbyul's Instagram account vanished, along with her tears and pain. Marigold – what a warm and cosy village. Suddenly, a thought flashed through her mind. Could it be that she'd been there before? She dug out an old family album and found a photo of herself, her younger sister and her mother, pregnant with her little brother, standing outside Our Snack Shop. Eunbyul gave a little start as she noticed the sign in the dated photo. She stroked the picture with a finger, fondly reminiscing about the old days. No wonder the neighbourhood had felt strangely familiar. That she'd found her way back to the village was no coincidence. It was fate.

Her family were beside themselves. Yet Eunbyul refused point blank to recover her account or to start a new one.

After talking it over with her lawyer, she decided to pay the full amount of compensation for breaking her advertising contracts and apologized to each individual who had bought shoddy products. With her income gone, her apartment was seized and sold at auction. As expected, her father's business ventures soon went bankrupt. His application to the court for relief was dismissed and he was jailed for two years for fraud. Just before the family's property was seized, Eunbyul sold her car and branded bags and arranged for her family to move to a two-room flat back in their old neighbourhood. Meanwhile, she applied for housing allowance for young adults living alone and got a tiny one-room for herself.

The fortune she'd amassed felt like a sandcastle. As if the moment you started thinking that the money would never run out, the pile of wealth would suddenly collapse to punish your arrogance. Looking at the shapeless debris left behind, Eunbyul's heart quietened. While her family was kicking up a fuss, insisting that she get back on Instagram, Eunbyul was at a loss to know what to do. Even if she were to return, she had absolutely no idea what she could upload or what captions to write. Had she really been an influencer and made all that money doing that for a living?

'I'm reaching the office. I have to work now. Let's sort out our problems for ourselves. Bye.'

At the end of the call, she slipped her headphones back on and turned on the noise cancellation mode. Should she block their numbers . . . Why was it so hard to cut ties with family? She stood at the traffic lights, staring at her phone, when suddenly she felt a light tap on her shoulder. It was her manager. Three months ago, Eunbyul had started working as a freelance home shopping merchandizer. So far, she'd been doing very well. Every product she brought in achieved higher sales than the last, and she enjoyed her work.

'Good morning!'

'Why are you so engrossed in your phone? Oh, never mind – I wanted to ask, how did you come up with such a great concept? Cream, sheet masks and a desk humidifier – the perfect combo for the dry season! The profit margin is high, and so is customer satisfaction. Did you know our team came out on top in the sales ranking?'

'Really? I'm so glad to hear that.'

Eunbyul smiled shyly and there was a spring in her step as she crossed the road. Even when it seemed that life was giving you the green light, a yellow or red light might appear out of nowhere, just as a red light that seemed to stretch on forever might turn green the next second. And back to red again. All we can do is keep walking and follow the changing lights. If it's not the colour we want, we pause. And when the light changes, it's time to resume our journey.

'Oh yeah, there's going to be an in-house opportunity for freelance merchandizers to switch to a permanent position. Managers can also put in a recommendation, and I'm thinking of submitting your name. What do you say?'

'I would really appreciate that. Thank you so much. I'll do my best.'

A green light. No doubt about it – a clear and bright green.

'Eunbyul, what do you usually do at the weekend?'

'I go to a hot spot or just relax for the day.'

'Oh . . . I thought you'd be working the whole time to come up with those great ideas.'

It was a Friday evening, and her colleague had asked her out of curiosity as they were leaving the office. Eunbyul was a permanent employee now and these days life was like wearing comfortable clothes that fit her perfectly. On her days off, she would cook delicious meals at home with her friends, or sometimes they would eat out at famous restaurants or visit a café. She kept an album full of their group photos. Outside work, she no longer bothered to put on make-up or wash her hair before going out. She'd put on her most comfortable clothes, wear a cap and be ready to leave the house. She enjoyed taking walks with no destination in mind. Her legs ached, but it made her notice things and places she hadn't seen before. Sometimes she would go for a jog. The dripping sweat, ragged breathing and her pounding heart reminded her that she was alive. In the past, there had barely been any times she'd felt truly *alive*.

While life was no bed of roses, there were many good moments. When her family reminisced about her heyday in the spotlight, instead of missing those days she shuddered at how lonely they sounded. Yet, there must have been great times, too. Maybe she should have kept those memories and erased only the painful bits? Sometimes she felt a tiny pang of regret. On days when such thoughts threatened to overwhelm her, she'd take out her notebook. Inside, she'd written down the wise words her friend had said on the day they'd met.

'Live your life. Don't think about cutting it short. As for the meaning or the fun in life, search for those after you've stopped thinking of death. And don't forget. You're good enough as you are. Instead of seeking some star in the sky, look for the one within yourself. Even when life is a little dark, your light remains bright.

'Remember. No matter what you choose to do, even if you're not dressed to impress but wearing clothes with a stain here and there, by simply existing in the world, you're shining like a star.'

Eonnie, I'm doing well. I miss you. I'll visit you soon. I wonder if that oppa passed his job interview. I want to write to you but I'm dozing off.

Her heavy eyelids fluttered to a close.

So sleepy . . . But it feels great to fall asleep . . . Today I'm alive . . . I'm glad. She yawned . . . *Everything else can wait till tomorrow.*

Slowly, she drifted off to sleep.

There was a real smile on her lips.

Chapter VI

HAE-IN

'Hae-in, what are your plans for this evening?'

'No plans. My work event ended early so I'm done for the day. Want to grab dinner?'

'Sounds good. Let's meet at seven at the laundry on the hill. Yeonhee is coming, too. Your hyung here has a major announcement to make! Ha ha ha.'

'Sounds like good news. Sure, let's meet at the laundry. But does it have food?'

'It's not just *any* laundry. You'll find out later. Bring something to share. A potluck party, OK? Ha ha ha.'

Hae-in smiled inwardly at the excitement colouring Jaeha's voice. Jaeha and Yeonhee had grown up together, while Hae-in had only moved into his grandmother's house in their neighbourhood in Grade 3, when he was ten. His mum, a photographer, had met his dad, a piano major, at a band performance where he played the keyboard. They'd fallen in love, and when

Hae-in was born, the three of them were a beautiful family. Heaven must have been jealous, because both his parents were forcibly taken away from him in a traffic accident. His grandmother became his guardian, and insurance money was paid out.

At his new school, quiet and introverted Hae-in was often alone. Jaeha, who'd noticed the new boy, started inviting him along to the playground. In no time, they were skipping rope, doing homework and spending lunch breaks together. When Jaeha introduced him to Yeonhee, the three of them became close. While they were like diaries to one another – no secret was too private – Hae-in was usually the listener. Whenever Jaeha and Yeonhee were talking, he would smile and listen quietly, keeping his thoughts to himself.

Having grown up alone, music was Hae-in's language. Chet Baker, Duke Ellington, Bill Evans and Paul Desmond were his favourites. In their performances, he found freedom. At university, Hae-in majored in art history. After graduation, he found a job as an exhibition planner, spending his free time taking photos, enjoying music and being a good listener. Hae-in was satisfied with life. He was doing what he enjoyed, and with ample time for hobbies, he privately thought that he was living rather lavishly.

As Hae-in's bus neared his stop, he ended the call and hit play on the next song: 'Take Five', an upbeat jazz number on the piano, drums and saxophone. Just being able to wind down the day with a song about taking a five-minute break made the never-ending groove of each day bleeding into the next seem much more bearable. Hae-in hummed the tune as he alighted.

'Bba ba bba bba, bbam bbam bba bam – bba ba bba bba, bbam bbam bba bbam.'

He slowly made his way up the steps to the top of the hill, his heart beating out the rhythm of the music. *Kung, kung, kung.*

'Phew, almost there. It's so nice to look out at everything from this high up.'

Hae-in raised the old Leica camera that hung around his neck and snapped several shots. He also took one of the two signs – the laundry and the snack shop – nestled side by side, and slowly walked around. The laundry stood at the edge of the highest vantage point of the seaside village. It looked like it had been built with lumber from a few hundred years ago, no – from a different time and space. Hae-in found the place oddly familiar.

I'm sure there's a staircase behind the garden that leads to the roof-top. Have I dreamed of this place? Why does it feel like I've been here before?

Hae-in circled round to the back, and there it was – the staircase. He climbed up to the rooftop. Even though it seemed no one else was around, he took care to keep his footsteps light. When he got to the top, he drew in a sharp breath.

What a place!

It was as if he'd reached the edge of the Earth. The sun loomed ahead of him, a fiery ball of red. A crisp autumn breeze sent the laundry on the clothes line fluttering. Like the sky, the clothes were also cast in a reddish hue, reminding him of petals dancing in the wind. *How ethereal.* On instinct, Hae-in raised his camera again and pressed the shutter.

From where he was standing, he could see the sea on two sides, and the city on the other two. It felt as if he'd crossed a boundary to an unknown place on Earth. Every item of clothing on the line was white. The wind blew them around and petals twirled out of the fabric, spiralling in the air. Against the setting sun, the petals danced.

Lost in beauty, Hae-in quickly snapped several shots. If there was a moment in life when he was sure that he'd never see anything more beautiful again, this was it. Through the viewfinder, his eyes trailed after the petals. He was absently zooming in for a close-up shot when he clicked his shutter once more, only to capture a shot of a tear balanced on the tip of a long eyelash.

. . . *What!*

Hae-in gave a little start and lowered the camera. He swallowed nervously. In his line of sight was a woman facing the setting sun. She appeared to be sending out the petals. Her palms were cupped and raised level with her shoulders, as if holding on to something extremely precious. Eyes closed, she murmured something under her breath before letting the petals go. The tears gathered at the tip of her lashes rolled down from the weight, gliding down her cheeks. As they touched the petals, there was a burst of light and the petals in flight vanished. Hae-in couldn't believe it. He rubbed his eyes with the other hand. The woman was still there; she was not a hallucination. The sun had gone down completely, leaving the last of its light lingering in the sky. Gently, it lit up a path for the night to stir from its slumber, as if hoping to keep it company.

The woman lowered her arms. She had yet to notice him. Hae-in pointed his camera discreetly at her. From behind, her silhouette seemed oddly familiar. The pattern on her dress formed a bouquet of petals, like the ones that had twirled out of the clothes and into the sky. The woman slowly turned and stared into Hae-in's camera. In the viewfinder, her eyes were deep-set, dark and full of sadness. Hae-in lowered his camera. He'd just witnessed something extraordinary. The woman was still crying. Taking careful steps, he walked towards her and blinked his eyes in surprise. She looked so much like his first love. He rubbed his eyes again, shaking his head as if trying to regain his senses.

'Hello. I apologize if I've startled you,' said Hae-in.

Jieun gave a little start. 'It's no problem.'

Wait. Why am I being so polite to this young man? Being so much older than anyone else around, Jieun had always been more comfortable speaking familiarly even to new acquaint-ances. Was this sudden burst of formality triggered because he had surprised her while she'd been crying?

'I'm Hae-in, a friend of Jaeha's. He told me to meet him here.'

'Ah, yes, he mentioned you'd be coming. I'm Jieun. I own this place. I've never let anyone see me doing this, though. Did I give you a shock?'

'Oh . . . no, not at all. But are you all right?'

'So rare that someone's asking after me. Yes, I'm fine.'

'It's OK to say you're not.'

'Do I look otherwise?'

'Hmm, yeah. You were crying as you bade the petals farewell.'

'Oh, so you've seen everything. And you've seen through how I'm pretending to be fine. Keep what you've witnessed today a secret, please. Although, aren't you curious about the petals appearing from the clothes?'

'I am, but let's leave that for next time. You look really pale right now. How about getting a warm drink and some rest? At this rate, you might get carried off on the wind too.'

Jieun chuckled and ran a hand through her hair. The stains removed from her visitors would dry into petals in the sun. By sending them off at sunset, when the sun was the brightest red, most of the petals would burn without leaving a trace. The ones left behind – the feelings, wounds and pain that still wouldn't disintegrate – would stay by Jieun's side, appearing whenever she used her powers. This man, Hae-in, had witnessed everything. But his mild-mannered attitude and his soothing voice quietened her heart. The look in his eyes reminded her of her father. Or a lover from one of her past lives. He smelled like nostalgia. They'd not spoken much, but already, she could tell that he was someone who respected others. To speak respectfully, be respectful, and be respected . . . *Is this what warmth and compassion are all about?* It had been a slip of the tongue, but on second thoughts, she liked the feeling of speaking formally. Perhaps she could consider doing so with the visitors at the laundry too.

'You're the one I loved and waited for most ardently.'

'Huh? Oh . . . er, me? Oh . . . thank you? But we've only just met . . .'

Seeing Hae-in flustered and blushing, Jieun burst out laughing. She couldn't help but tease him a little.

'That's the flower language of the red camellia. The petals you saw. I send them off, praying that people can love life again once their pain and wounds are completely erased. That's why

I do it at sunset, when the petals will be able to burn with fervour.'

Hae-in listened attentively. Seeing how the colour had returned to Jieun's cheeks, he breathed a sigh of relief. *Why am I so concerned?* They barely knew each other. Was it because she reminded him of his first love? No, she was far more charismatic, drawing people in with her enigmatic charm. The two of them stood in the eye of the whirlpool of petals, which seemed to be looking on in awe at how Jieun was learning how to open up.

'Aren't they beautiful? They change colour according to my mood, but usually they're red. It's more comfortable to keep my emotions in check. Oh, look at me. I've said too much . . .'

Was it because she'd just cried? Or that she was keen to continue the conversation with this stranger? Whatever the reason, her heart was much calmer now. Come to think of it, he was being oddly nonchalant about having witnessed her powers. Was this his talent? To get people to open up so easily?

If he were a colour, he would be a gentle beige.

Jieun was reminded of the beige blanket she'd had as a child. It had been a while since she'd last reminisced about an item she'd left behind. She was about to walk past Hae-in to head downstairs when she paused and turned.

'By the way, the photos won't turn out. I can't be captured on camera. I'm going down, are you going to stay here?'

Hae-in watched the woman straighten her back, push down her shoulders and draw herself up to her full height. She claimed to be fine, but her shaky voice betrayed her. Hae-in trailed behind her in silence. They walked down the spiral stairs to the bar table on the ground floor. A different staircase from the one Hae-in had walked up.

'Oh? You two were together up there? Looks like you've already met. This is Hae-in, my friend!'

Yeonhee unpacked the three-tier dosirak that had just been delivered. Jieun greeted Yeonhee with a nod, smiling as she moved behind the bar table to prepare the tea. A moment later, Jaeha burst through the door.

'I got the job! A permanent position, finally! Now I get to have the insurance coverage all the full-time workers enjoy! Ha ha ha!'

'What? You got the job? Wow, amazing! Congrats!'

Yeonhee jumped up from her seat, the dosirak forgotten. Because she had borne witness to how hard and long Jaeha had struggled to balance his dreams with reality, her happiness was tinged with a little sadness. He'd once had so much love for movies, but since he'd come back from the mind laundry, he no longer so much as mentioned the word. Instead, he turned his focus towards finding a stable, permanent job that came with employment insurance. Yeonhee suspected that the pain he'd erased was his filmmaking days. But even if he no longer remembered, she'd treasure those memories for him. His passion for movies, and how he'd shone.

In a few big strides, Hae-in relieved Jaeha of the fried chicken he was holding and gave him a bear hug.

'Congrats, Jaeha. You've worked hard.'

He thumped Jaeha twice on the back before letting him go.

'I'm here to remind Jieun to eat dinner, but it looks like there's a gathering?'

The ajumma from the snack shop next door smiled at the visitors. She set down the black plastic bag in front of Jieun at the bar table and looked around. *Wait, two rolls aren't enough to go round.*

'Come and join us. There's so much food.'

'Aigoo, you all go ahead. I've eaten a fistful of barley rice with yeolmu kimchi and two rounds of sesame oil. I came to check on Jieun sajangnim in case she hadn't eaten all day but I'm glad to see you all. If you need fish cake soup, come over. Have fun! I'll be off.'

'Ajumma, thank you,' said Jieun, picking up a piece of kimbap.

It felt good to be surrounded by people. Yet she couldn't help being nervous. By letting them into her heart, she was basically starting a countdown to the time they'd have to part. Now that she was on her supposed last life, she was learning to let go of her wariness and the barriers she'd put up in her heart. But there was a seed of doubt inside her. Would this truly be the last life? Could she then die like everyone else? These people would die, but maybe not her. Then one day, she'd be all alone again, grieving her losses. She didn't want to get hurt, so she'd always fled before getting close to anyone. It had been a long, long time since she'd had dreams and hopes. And knots in her stomach.

Can't I live a life without anxiety?

As she mulled it over, she rinsed the teacups with hot water from the kettle, to help the cups retain the warmth of the tea. She'd learned that there was an optimal temperature for everything, but the requirements for the tea and the teacups were different. The teacups needed boiling water, but to avoid scalding the drinker, the tea itself should be brewed at a lower temperature.

'I'll take the cups over to the other table.'

'Oh, they're hot to the touch. Please, don't use your bare hands.'

Jaeha and Yeonhee spun round, flabbergasted. Were their ears playing tricks on them?

'Er . . . did Sajangnim just speak politely to Hae-in? She actually knows how?'

'Um . . . I-I . . . Since when? That didn't come out right.'

Turning her back to their gaping faces, Jieun poured out the tea and in her usual casual way told Hae-in: 'Take these over.'

'Oh yeah, that's the sajangnim we know. Impossible for her to be all formal and polite. I'm hungry, let's tuck in.'

'Let's eat. Eat to live, live to eat. Fill our stomachs and our lives!'

'That's right. Today's a great day! Let's set aside our worries for now and have fun.'

'If the number *ten* represents a whole life, then a happy day would allow us to endure the other nine days of unhappiness.'

'Sajangnim. What are you thinking about so intently on the rooftop every evening?' Yeonhee asked, her cheeks bulging with kimbap.

After the lesson with Jieun, Yeonhee was finding it easier to smile even when dealing with customers who were a pain in the ass, or when she missed her bus by three stops. She did occasionally think that her forced smile in the mirror looked like the Joker, but ever since she'd resolved to smile more often, she'd found some peace. The first time she'd glimpsed sadness flickering over Jieun's face, it had bothered her to think that Jieun looked like this whenever she was alone.

'Why are you so curious?'

'It's nothing. Just that when I see you keeping still and facing the sunset, it feels like you're going to be sucked into the twilight. It's OK if you don't want to tell us! Heh heh.' Yeonhee smiled shyly, scratching her head in embarrassment.

Jieun nodded twice and chewed her lip. After a moment, she decided to speak up.

'Um . . . I was praying for the peace and wellbeing of others. It's as though I'm lighting candles in my heart.'

'What do you mean – candles in your heart?'

'We light candles in prayer, right? And in the same way that the candle burns to give light to its surroundings, when the sun is setting and burning bright I pray for the wellbeing of those who've crossed paths with the laundry. Even before I settled down here, I was brewing healing tea and helping to lighten the pains in others' hearts.'

'Wow, you've been running the laundry for a long time!'

'A very long time indeed. All of us . . . we need at least one person to believe in us and to cheer us on.'

'. . . Only one?'

'Yeah, one who truly has faith in us. It's not easy to find that person. Which is why I want to be that person for others. By keeping them in my thoughts, I hope that they'll gain the strength to keep going in life.'

They let her words steep in their thoughts: how she was always thinking of others, how she refused to charge for her services, only asked that they pass on kindness. *What was it that had led her to this neighbourhood?*

Jaeha was the one who broke the silence.

'Hae-in, let's put on some music. Sajangnim, this dude chooses the sickest tunes.'

Hae-in stirred from his reverie and raised his eyebrows in acknowledgement.

'Here. We can connect it via Bluetooth,' said Yeonhee, taking out a speaker from her bag.

There was an easy familiarity about their interactions.

Jieun stood up to prepare a fresh pot of tea. Music flowed in the background while she waited for the water to boil. *Blub blub.* As ever, it took time for the water to reach its optimal temperature. When the water was ready for the tea, she came to the table and turned to Hae-in.

'Chet Baker's "Autumn Leaves"? Perfect for an autumn night like this.'

'Bingo. You listen to him, too?'

'I do. His songs have a touch of anxiety running alongside passion and excitement. Youth. That's what it reminds me of.'

'Youth . . . That's fitting. Do you have a favourite music genre?'

'I like everything. I used to know Chet well. I wonder how his music would have been different if he hadn't done drugs and had lived a happy life.'

'Oh.'

'Are you shocked that I knew him? Are you thinking: *What a weird woman. She must be dreaming?*'

'Not really. Somehow it makes sense that you were once close to Chet Baker, Jieun-ssi.'

'I had a friend who played in a band so we often went to watch gigs. I wanted to help Chet, too, but doing so felt like it'd shake the foundation of his music. Sometimes suffering can turn into strength, or fuel for creative inspiration.'

Hae-in was usually sparing with words in the company of someone new. Jaeha gaped at Hae-in and Jieun, his eyes swivelling between the two of them. And when Hae-in said *Jieun-ssi*, Jaeha broke out into fits of giggles as he elbowed his friend.

'Dude, what's with *Jieun-ssi*? You should call her *Sajangnim*!'

'But that's so stiff and formal,' Hae-in said.

There was a gentle firmness when he spoke that would make you nod in agreement. Even something unfathomable seemed logical when Hae-in said it.

'Oh . . . In that case, should we all call her *Jieun-ssi* – ouch! Lee Yeonhee, stop pinching me!'

'Don't be dense, Yoo Jaeha, grow up! Don't butt in where you don't belong.'

They were thirty-three years old, but in the company of childhood friends, they still behaved like children. Or rather, they longed to remain young at heart. As they laughed, sharing food and drink, Jieun looked on in envy at their camaraderie. She felt a sharp stab of loneliness thinking about how the friends would grow old together. *Me, too. I also want to grow old with all of you.*

Yeonhee turned back to Hae-in.

'Hae-in, this laundry can help you to remove the stains on your heart or iron out crumpled feelings. If you've something you want to erase, this is your chance.'

'A stain on the . . . heart?'

'You know, like: *I wish I could let go of this misery.* Don't you have moments like that?'

'Often.'

'Then get Sajangnim to help you.'

Hae-in reached for his teacup. He took a small sip, and another, searching for the next song to play. *He's retreating into himself. I'd better stop pushing him*, Yeonhee thought to herself. It was Hae-in's habit to fall into silence whenever he didn't want to continue the conversation. He had his reasons for keeping quiet, so they respected his silence. Instead of probing, they'd remain by his side when he was having a hard time. This was their unspoken rule.

'Jaeha. Is your mother happy that you found a job?'

This time, Jieun broke the silence. On the day they'd first met, Jaeha had implored her to erase his mother's pain instead of his own. Since then, Jieun had been waiting with a candle lit in her heart.

'I called her on the way here, and she was laughing in delight at the news.'

'Of course, how proud she must be. Did she mention when she was coming by?'

'She said she'd make lots of delicious food and visit me some time next week. Can I bring her here?'

'Definitely. You haven't forgotten the opening special I gave you, right?'

'Oooh, Sajangnim! You remembered! Of course I didn't. I'll bring her!'

Jaeha was grateful that Jieun hadn't forgotten her promise to help his mother. He wanted to thank her, but out of shyness he tried to convey his feelings by filling Jieun's empty plate with the fruits that Yeonhee brought. As he added a generous portion to her plate, his eyes landed on the patterns on her dress. He tilted his head quizzically.

'Sajangnim. Do you own several dresses with similar prints?'

'You mean this? Nope, it's my only one.'

'Eh? Really? I remembered seeing more flowers on it.'

The three of them turned to gaze at the floral embroidery on her dress. Jieun, too, looked down. *No way would the number of flowers ever decrease. It only ever increased year by year.*

'That's impossible. Jaeha, you must be tired today. Come on, all of you. It's time to go. I need to open the shop.'

'It doesn't seem like anyone's coming today. Why don't you just pack up and head home early? You look tired.'

Jieun's eyes crinkled into a smile. Had they already got close enough to be asking after one another and noticing when someone seemed tired? She'd planned to journey through this life without leaving anything or anyone behind, but it looked like that wouldn't happen. Each time she found people precious to her, she wanted to protect them. But this made goodbyes difficult. To be able to age naturally would be such a blessing.

'All right, once you've finished cleaning up, go on home. I'll be in the laundry room.'

Jieun headed upstairs, and in her mind she was already awaiting the next customer on their way to her with a bruised and battered heart. Hae-in's gaze lingered on her thin, frail frame. What did it mean – removing stains of the heart? Ironing out feelings? And who was she – this woman with such deep sadness? Long after Jieun had gone upstairs, Hae-in's eyes rested on the staircase, looking deep in thought.

Chapter VII

YEONJA

I want to live well. Yeonja wasn't quite sure what that meant, but she'd thought she'd be happy with just an ordinary life. However, at an early age, she had realized how tremendously difficult it was to live like other people. If only the reality hadn't hit her so soon.

'Yeonja, about your university tuition fees . . .'

Her frail, elderly father clenched and unclenched his fist, his hunched back turned to Yeonja. Father was always anxious and jittery. Despite being a decade older than her mother, he was terrible at being the head of the household. His only talent was getting her mother pregnant.

As her family grew in number over the years, Yeonja knew what was awaiting her. Topping her class meant nothing at all. She wasn't going to university. The moment she came of age, the responsibility of caring for her five siblings would fall on her. She was all too aware, yet she continued to pour her soul into her studies. Life in that insufferable household would have been unbearable otherwise.

'Father, I will not go to university.'

He didn't ask why. In the kitchen, her mother's hands paused while washing the rice, but she, too, remained silent. There was no point asking *why*, not when everything had already been decided.

Yeonja swept past her second and third siblings and returned to her room. She quickly packed a duffel bag and, without saying a word, left home. Her older friend, Jungsoon eonnie, had already started working at the industrial complex. Yeonja was going to join her at the production line of a tofu factory. Just one year. She'd work for a year and save up for university. Just one year.

'Yeonja, why didn't you eat before leaving? The rice is warm – I've just cooked it. How's the room? Is it too cold? Comfortable?'

'Um . . . not bad . . . Jungsoon eonnie and I share a room at the dorm. I'm eating well here.'

'Good,' said her mum, pausing. 'You need to have proper meals . . . Sorry I can't do much for you . . .'

Her mother's sigh was deep and heavy. Yeonja felt a pressure crushing her chest, suffocating her.

'It's OK. I'll send some money once I get paid.'

'I feel bad . . . We'll try to manage.'

'How? I thought Father couldn't work with his injured arm? I'll send money for the time being.'

'Thank you . . .'

Her mother had a good heart, but she was powerless. And with her father working as a day labourer at construction sites all his life, they had always lived in poverty. The family ate out only once a year, always at Christmas and always at the Chinese restaurant. Seven bowls of jajangmyeon and a serving of white rice. They couldn't even afford to order enough for everyone. Her growing siblings were always hungry. They wolfed down the food in no time, not forgetting to lick up the last bit of sauce. Watching them, Yeonja would push her bowl their way and munch on the yellow pickled radish served on the side instead. She chewed on it for as long as she could, and when washed down with water, the salty taste made her feel somewhat full.

She was sick and tired of being poor. If only she could escape the dreariness of her reality, and the stench of poverty that clung to their house. *There must be a better life out there.* The thought took root in her, crystallizing into *hope*.

'Yeonja. There's a staff lunch today. Let's go.'

The moment Yeonja ended the call, Jungsoon slipped her arm into hers, chattering away. Jungsoon was pretty. And after she'd started working, she changed her style. She got her ears pierced and permed her hair at the salon. She also swapped her wardrobe for miniskirts, and often wore large earrings and a full face of make-up. At her invitation, Yeonja smiled faintly and shook her head. It would only be a year. She had no interest in hanging out with the other factory workers. *I won't stay for long*, she reminded herself. She would save up her wages and go to university, graduate, find a job, get married to an average man and have just one kid. She didn't have a preference – son or daughter would be fine. She imagined their family of three living in a small apartment, going on holidays occasionally, and if they went to a Chinese restaurant, they'd be able to order jajangmyeon for everyone and even add a plate of tangsuyuk. An ordinary life – this was her dream. But this was also the hardest thing in the world: to live an ordinary life like others.

'Yeonja, did you use perfume today?'

'Eh? No, I don't have any.'

'Really? But you smell different. It's nice.'

Jungsoon rested her head on Yeonja's shoulder and sniffed at her affectionately. Ever since she was young, Jungsoon had had a keen sense of smell. She could even figure out the dinner menu from the corridor.

'Oh . . . I used a new soap today,' said Yeonja shyly. Jungsoon lifted her head and let out a little chuckle.

'See? I was right. Something is different today. I remember things by their smells. From now on, I'm going to think of you together with this smell. Mmmm . . . what a nice scent. Like a baby. Can I also use the soap?'

'Um, sure. Go ahead.'

'Yay! Then you're free to use my make-up sometimes!'

Yeonja nodded. Some people are kind. Warm. Sincere and pure, and therefore impossible to hate. Able to put everyone around them at ease. Jungsoon was exactly like that.

'Eonnie . . . where's lunch today?'

'Probably Chinese?'

'Chinese? . . . Hmm, should I go?'

'Yes! Of course! Let's go.'

'Perhaps this is what it means to live an ordinary life,' Yeonja muttered to herself as she gazed up at the sky. It was cloudless and unusually blue.

'Ajumoni. One jajangmyeon each. And for every table, a big serving of tangsuyuk and palbochae.'

Twenty-plus workers gathered at the Chinese restaurant for lunch. The factory foreman would sometimes treat the staff to a meal, but never out of his own pocket. *He looks like a young master from a rich family. What's he doing as the factory foreman?* Yeonja sometimes wondered. But she never asked. As long as she didn't, there'd be no conversations, and with no interactions, she'd be able to steer clear of misunderstandings and conflicts. Getting close to people and being entangled in their affairs would only cause headaches. Just like asking herself why she'd ended up staying for three years instead of one. As her thoughts dwelled on her father's mounting medical fees, incurred since his hospitalization last month, she deftly mixed the jajangmyeon and slurped a huge mouthful, stuffing in a crispy piece of tangsuyuk.

'Yeonja-ssi, no one is fighting you for the food. You'll choke if you eat like that. Take your time. Ajumoni, bring us a bottle of soda, please.'

Yeonja could only cough in response with all the food lodged in her throat. The foreman thumped her gently on the back and passed her a paper napkin.

'Ah . . . thank you.'

The foreman laughed. 'I'm guessing you like Chinese food. You only join our lunches when the menu is Chinese,' he said, handing her the soda.

'Er . . . right.'

Yeonja was surprised. Like he'd said, she only joined them when they were eating Chinese. She hated company lunches, but she liked how she could have a whole bowl of jajangmyeon to herself, not to mention the tangsuyuk. Several people had given her the side-eye for missing team lunches, but she didn't care. She'd be gone this time next year. *But he noticed that I like Chinese food.* His words created a ripple in her heart.

'That's why I've been choosing to come here for the past few lunches. It means Yeonja-ssi will join us and it's great to have all of us here,' he laughed heartily.

She gave him a polite nod and continued slurping her noodles. The noodles would start to clump if she was too slow. The crispy tangsuyuk was also best enjoyed piping hot. She'd been trying to save money by eating only at the dormitory canteen, so this was her only chance to eat out. *He must be the considerate type who's good at looking after others . . .* Yeonja eyed the palbochae on the table as she chewed her tangsuyuk.

It was midday when they finished their meal. Yeonja squinted in the brightness of the summer sun. It was a blazing hot July. The foreman offered her a paper cup of hot coffee. Just as Yeonja was deciding whether or not to accept it, he spoke.

'You don't like coffee? After jajangmyeon, some instant coffee will hit the spot.' He laughed again.

'Oh . . . OK. Thank you.'

It was the kind of summer afternoon where even standing still would leave you sweating buckets. Yeonja took the cup, flustered. She didn't like coffee. To develop a liking for such a frivolous luxury was nothing but a waste of money. Instead of putting herself in a situation where she'd be upset that she couldn't afford to satisfy her cravings, it would be much better not to like it in the first place. No expectations, no disappointments. Yeonja was someone who was too used to giving up rather than seeking more.

But why was the foreman trying to make conversation with her? How awkward.

'I haven't seen you talk to the others at all. Yeonja-ssi, what do you like to do on your days off?'

'I . . . oh, nothing much.'

'How about watching a movie with me this week?'

'. . .'

Yeonja, who'd never been to the cinema, was at a loss for words.

'I'd treat you to your favourite jajangmyeon and tangsuyuk,' he said, laughing again.

After getting a 'yes' from Yeonja, the foreman let out his signature hearty laugh and walked away. Meanwhile, beads of sweat were rolling down Yeonja's face. Even her palms were damp, softening the paper cup. Only then did she take a small sip of the coffee.

Under the blazing sun, Yeonja stood unmoving. Yet it was as though her body was going to cook. It was that kind of summer.

Bam bam bam! Bam bam bam! Bam bam bam!

At the persistent pounding on the door early in the morning, Yeonja stirred awake. Since that lunch, she'd spent all her rest days with the foreman, watching movies and eating jajangmyeon and tangsuyuk, until one day she found out that she was pregnant. They moved into a rented room near the factory, but because he needed to take care of his sickly mother, he would stay over at his parents' place about four days a week.

Had he forgotten his keys? Yeonja dragged herself, heavily pregnant, out of bed. The moment she opened the door, it was as if she was struck by a bolt of lightning, knocking her head to the side. Her cheek smarted. *What the hell is going on?*

'You bitch. How dare you seduce my husband and end up pregnant! You slut! Was it all planned? You'd find work at the factory and then throw yourself at my man?'

The woman was exploding in front of her like firecrackers, but Yeonja felt somehow removed from it all. What on earth was she talking about? She rubbed her temples, reeling from the slap.

'Could you please explain what's going on? I think you've got the wrong address.'

'The factory foreman living with you is my husband! And we have two kids!'

The force of her words knocked Yeonja back. The world was spinning as she found herself roughly shoved out of the way. Stepping inside, the woman unleashed her rage on the few possessions around the room. Misfortune and accidents – couldn't Yeonja have got a warning before everything came crashing down? Why wasn't it possible to know what lay ahead so that she could avoid it? Even if she was meant to suffer, shouldn't she be allowed to brace herself? Did misfortune feed on misery?

On several occasions since she'd been with the foreman, an inexplicable sense of unease had grazed her heart; she often had a nagging feeling that something was wrong, but she had never thought to ask. He'd simply told her that his mother was ill and suggested that they push back the marriage registration and their wedding ceremony until their child was born. *But, what? A married man? Impossible. What about the child in my womb? Our child?*

She felt a surge of warmth between her legs. It seemed like the child wanted to assert its presence even then. When the fuming woman noticed the mix of water and blood flowing from between Yeonja's legs, she shrieked.

'Oh my god! Your waters have broken! Shit, where's that jerk? I can't believe this, seriously!'

The two women stared at each other. Yeonja knew that the only person in the world who could save her right now was the woman in front of her – the woman with whom she was unknowingly sharing a man. Unable to stand, she cradled her belly and sank down to her knees.

'I'm sorry . . . but the baby is coming out . . . Help me . . . please.'

Yeonja felt her consciousness slipping away. The child . . . She'd have to protect her child. *Protect my child.* She felt as if her body were being ripped apart and, in her agony, an old memory came rushing to the surface. A memory so painful that for a long time it had lain forgotten, buried.

★

'Yeonja, eat this. I'll be back soon.'

That day, Mum had dressed her in her best clothes and braided her hair. At the crowded train station, she bought Yeonja some milk and bread and told her to wait. There was an air of finality about her mother that day, as if she'd come to a decision. Mum let go of her hands, but Yeonja could feel her touch lingering. It was possible, if you really loved someone, to sense their emotions even from the tips of their fingers. Mum's fingertips were weeping. Little Yeonja wanted to ask, but the question wouldn't escape her lips. Her mother had always seemed sad, but today, she looked calm.

Yeonja clutched her doll tight and watched her mother disappear into the crowd before tears started to roll down her cheeks. She didn't dare to cry out, so she wept silently and drank her milk. *I'll have to save the bread*, Yeonja thought. Mum wouldn't be returning soon. Instinct told five-year-old Yeonja that she would likely not come back for a long, long time. Children are sensitive to emotions; they just know. Finally, tired out from the tears, she fell asleep in the waiting room.

'Yeonja, it's Mummy. I'm so sorry, my poor child. Mummy is sorry she kept you waiting . . . Sorry . . .'

Late at night, the empty waiting room was pitch black. Her mother pulled the sleeping child into her arms and wept. Hot tears rolled down her cheeks. Yeonja stirred awake and only then did she finally burst into tears of her own. A warm sensation rushed out from her crotch, flowing between her legs. She'd forced herself to keep it in, afraid that her mother might return in the short time she had gone to the bathroom. *Why did you come back?* Her mum was also dressed nicely for once. Yeonja had questions, but she couldn't bring herself to ask any. All she could do was grip her mum's hands tightly and wail. Loudly.

After that day, Yeonja never cried out again.

'Wake up! Let's get you to the hospital. You can't possibly give birth here. How am I supposed to deliver it? Shit, shit, shit – this is really happening!'

The woman – her husband's wife – was yelling at Yeonja, trying to help her. *My husband's wife is me. It's me . . .* Yeonja wrapped her hands around her belly and endured the searing pain, praying that the warmth slipping out from between her legs wasn't her child. *Life can't be this unfair. It just can't.* She faded into blackness.

When winter descends on our hearts, the reason we can endure it is because of the hope that this season, too, will pass. *Hope* – it can breathe life into us. Or summon death. What keeps us alive is the hope that spring will come around again, bringing with it the blazing summer followed by the cool autumn. If we can't keep the faith, how are we to endure life?

At the entrance to the laundry where she and Jaeha had agreed to meet, Yeonja paused. The camellias in their full glory reminded her of hope. *I didn't know camellias could bloom in October*, she mused. She picked up some fallen petals and, for a moment, stared at them resting in her palm.

'So beautiful. So gorgeous. I wonder if Jaeha has seen these?'

Yeonja fished out her phone and snapped a photo of the

petals. She took a few more shots of the flowers nearby and sent them to Jaeha. When you love someone, you think of them immediately when you see something beautiful, or when you're eating something delicious. *Jaeha.* Saying his name aloud made her chest ache. *My beloved child.* Yeonja let her gaze wander. It had been a long time since she'd returned to this neighbourhood. Filling her lungs with the briny seaside air, she thought back to the days she'd lived here with Jungsoon.

After she'd given birth to Jaeha, the man only visited once a month. Soon it stretched to every two months, and one day he finally packed up and left. He didn't look back, not even when the four-year-old Jaeha held on to the hem of his jeans and refused to let go. He was abandoning them for a better life. He didn't want to be tied down to a crammed room that didn't even have its own toilet. She watched him leave, her mouth pressed shut.

To survive, she worked whatever odd jobs she could find – making side dishes at a restaurant, cleaning houses, working in the factory – until one day Jungsoon found her at the restaurant where she was working.

'Yeonja! How did you end up like this . . . ? What happened?'

A month later, Yeonja moved to the seaside village where Jungsoon was living, here in Marigold. In the years that they'd lost contact, Jungsoon had quit the factory job and gone on to complete a beautician course. For a while, she worked in a salon before opening her own shop here in Marigold. She'd been living alone in a small house she'd bought with her earnings, so she offered a room to Yeonja and Jaeha. After they settled down, Yeonja got a job making side dishes at a nearby restaurant, and at home she took over the housework. With her skilled hands, she could make delicious food even with few ingredients. Together, she and Jungsoon raised Jaeha. Fed warm meals in a warm house, Jaeha had started to thrive and put on weight.

The day Jungsoon passed away of late-stage cancer, Yeonja wanted to follow her. But because she had Jaeha, she needed to live on. The day she first held Jaeha in her arms, she knew that she'd lost her freedom to die by her own hand.

The luxury to ponder the meaning of life was never hers. She lived because she had been born and being alive meant she'd continue to live day by day. Yeonja had no idea how she'd survived through everything. It was all in the past now, but occasionally, when the memories washed up, they were as vivid as though they were only yesterday.

Jungsoon eonnie's house used to be down that back street behind the hill, she thought. Would it still be there?

'Well, if this isn't Yeonja! Are you well? It's been a long time! How are you still so beautiful?'

'Gosh! Ajumoni, hello! You haven't changed a bit yourself. How've you been?'

'Yeah, well, aching here and there. Nothing too serious, so it's fine. At our age, life is about tending to our ailing body. Jaeha has been dropping by my place recently. Are you here to see him?'

The ajumma from the snack shop had dragged herself out on her bad leg to go grocery shopping and was just about to return to her shop when she spotted Yeonja. Her gnarled hands covered Yeonja's, which were also beginning to wrinkle. The warmth exchanged through their palms was deeper than any words.

'Yeah, just busy getting through each day. Jaeha told me to meet him at the laundry. He's always told me not to visit, but it seems now he's missing me. He phoned yesterday, and I came running.'

Jaeha had moved out for university, then moved again when he decided to switch schools and make films, and after several more moves here and there as he tried to live the life he wanted independently of his mother, he'd eventually settled down in this seaside village. After all, it was where they'd both felt at their happiest and most at ease.

'That's great. The door is open, so you can wait inside. Jieun sajangnim is a good person. You should meet her.'

'I will. Jaeha told me she serves really delicious tea, and to have some while waiting for him to get off work. He said he'd arranged everything.'

'Aigoo, that boy. Always keen to share good stuff with his mother. Still the same after all these years. When they got Choco Pies at school, all his classmates would be munching theirs on the spot, but he'd put his in his bag to share it with you. Such a sweet child. Aigoo, why am I tearing up? I must be feeling my age. Yes, be on your way, and remember to come by for lunch later, all right?'

'OK, thank you.'

Wiping her tears with her apron, the ajumma shuffled back to her shop. Yeonja walked towards the door of the laundry. Beside her, crimson flower petals rustled to line the path for her. Her eyes rounded in surprise at the carpet of red swirling by her feet. *A breeze of petals, a flower road.*

'Where did you all come from? How pretty . . .'

The petals turned cartwheels at her feet, as if urging her to walk along the red carpet they'd prepared for her. She'd never seen such a gorgeous display. Yeonja followed the path, pushing open the door to the laundry.

The moment she touched the door, it swung open. Jieun greeted her as if she'd been waiting. Yeonja's gaze landed on Jieun's smooth forehead, and then her bright smile. She gasped. For a split second, she thought she was looking at Jungsoon. Jieun put her palms together and greeted Yeonja politely.

'Welcome. This is the Marigold Mind Laundry, where we remove stains and iron out the wrinkles from your heart.'

The petals continued to flutter in circles around the two women. From the back of the laundry, Jaeha quietly observed Yeonja's joy at seeing the petals dance. There were also some swirling petals beside him. He spoke to them.

'I'll leave her in your good hands. That's my mother, Ms Yeonja – the person I love most in the world.'

The petals piled up joyfully, one upon the other, before flying off, as though acknowledging his request. He watched them make their way to the front of the laundry before he turned around in the direction of the beach. He broke into a run, heading toward the embrace of the sea. The waters carried many stories. The sea held people's secrets, swallowing them with the waves. And that was why the sea was deep, so deep.

'Make yourself comfortable while I prepare the tea. Would hot tea be all right?'

Yeonja, who was about to come in alongside the petals, was hovering at the entrance. Unaccustomed to such warm hospitality, her first reaction was to put her guard up. But she remembered that Jaeha had told her this was a very nice place, and so it must be. She clutched her shoulder bag with both hands and sat down on the chair nearest to the door.

To give Yeonja space, Jieun took her time preparing the tea. The same way that some people take to unfamiliar situations with ease, others might be wary or afraid. Over the lifetimes she'd been brewing the healing tea, Jieun had learned the ways to respect boundaries and give ample time and space for the other person to feel at ease.

Yeonja slowly took in the interior. Calm piano music was playing. She recognized the tune as Hae-in's favourite. Whenever he used to come over to their house, the boys would listen to it together. Carefully, she placed her bag on the chair next to her. It was quiet, but the silence wasn't at all uncomfortable.

Jieun prepared the tea with care and carried it over. Taking a deep breath, Yeonja prepared to speak.

'Good afternoon. Jaeha told me about this place. He always has such a vivid imagination, I thought he just wanted to add some colour to the tale, but it seems like this really is a laundry service with a unique concept?'

Jieun set down the cups carefully. She smiled and nodded, casting her eyes down as she poured the tea. Yeonja appeared to be in her fifties. Her hair was tied up neatly, and she wore a white knit shirt and a pair of comfortable black slacks with a beige cotton jacket. Her face was unadorned and nondescript. But her small hands, which should have looked elegant, were coarse and callused. Jieun waited for her to sip her tea. Half a cup should ease her up a little. Sometimes knowing how to respect a person's time and space could offer more comfort than any magic.

'I don't usually drink tea, but this is good . . .'

Yeonja's wariness slowly dissipated, giving way to a shy smile. Jieun walked out from behind the bar table and sat down beside her, leaving a chair in between them. She thought Yeonja would be more comfortable if they weren't facing each other.

Yeonja's jacket was now folded neatly and placed on top of her bag. She even unwound her scarf. *It's time*, Jieun thought.

'This is a healing tea that's only available at the mind laundry. It's my special recipe. Would you like another cup?'

'Oh, sure. But is it OK if I'm here drinking tea for free?'

'It's fine. Jaeha got a job at a great company, didn't he? He said he'd pay for the tea.'

At the mention of her son, Yeonja smiled with pride. Jieun poured her another cup of tea, and this time Yeonja looked more relaxed. She took a sip, staring in front of her as she spoke.

'I haven't been back to Marigold for a long time. Jaeha told me he hoped I would find some comfort here. It's strange, but I do feel much more at ease now. Thank you.'

Jieun slid into the seat next to her, closing the distance between them. Gently, she set down a white t-shirt next to Yeonja.

'Each and every one of us has our own wounds of different sizes and shapes, but somehow our own pain always seems magnified. Don't you think erasing some memories, or smoothing your feelings could help a little? Jaeha says he hopes to wipe away the hurt in your heart. If you would put on this t-shirt and head up to the first floor, you may close your eyes and think back to those moments you wish to forget. After you pass the shirt back to me, I'll wash it clean for you.'

'Jaeha said that? My darling boy . . . he shouldn't be fretting over this. He's still a child, he should be more carefree . . .'

Yeonja cradled the t-shirt in her arms. Tears pooled in her eyes. *My mature, sensitive child.* Jaeha was always behaving like the adult between the two of them, taking care of her when he was the child. But this had always gutted Yeonja. When Jaeha, who had never so much as whined for a piece of candy before, had declared that he wanted to make movies, she was secretly pleased.

Yeonja sighed.

'Things I want to forget . . . There are many, of course. Too many. I don't even know where to start. They say time is the best medicine – I hate to admit it, but it's true. Things were so tough in the moments I experienced them, but when time passed they were simply events in the past. More than the moments that I actually want to erase, there are moments so painful they still make my heart ache.'

'What kind of moments?'

'Jaeha was still very young when the landlord suddenly gave us a month's eviction notice. But it was already the cheapest place in the entire neighbourhood. I had no choice but to take up another restaurant job at night. There was nowhere I could send Jaeha, so for the first few nights I'd take him to work with me. The dirty looks I got from the restaurant owners! But how could you expect a young child to sit still next to his mother who's doing the dishes? I had no choice. For about a month, before we ended up moving here with Jungsoon eonnie, I left him at home and chained the door shut. Do you know how much energy a young boy has? I couldn't possibly tie him to me on a leash as I worked, and if I'd left him alone he was sure to venture out and lose his way. At that time, losing Jaeha was my worst nightmare. A five-year-old child wouldn't know how to return home. You can't imagine how much it pained me to leave him in the room and lock him up . . . Every step away from him felt so heavy when I could hear him wailing from inside . . . Day after day, separated by a door, we'd both cry . . .'

Jieun said nothing but reached out to grasp Yeonja's hands. At the warmth of her touch, Yeonja simply let her tears flow. She wept quietly.

'The poor thing must have known, because he suddenly went silent after a few days. Even when his lips were trembling, he held it in . . . That broke my heart, and I cried even harder as I walked away. If I'd sobbed in front of him, how upset he would've been.

'At this age, I've come to realize that children are much stronger than their parents. And I knew that I'd be imposing on Jungsoon eonnie, but I had no choice. She was like the sunshine in my life – warm, bright and full of laughter.'

A faint smile played on her lips. Whenever Yeonja had felt bad for troubling her, Jungsoon eonnie would wave off her apology.

'Yeonja-yah,' she would say. 'Girls like us who grew up unloved have to band together. We aren't like those people who were showered with affection – so shining and flawless. We're the shadows. If we get too close to the light, we'll burn up. I don't want that. So, let's be shade and shelter for each other. I've burned myself on love one too many times. I'm sick of it. Marriage? No way. Stay by my side. I'm lonely, I need you more than you need me.'

Stay by my side. I need you. Nobody had ever told Yeonja that before. Jungsoon's words were supposed to be comforting, but Yeonja was devastated to hear them. Jungsoon was like the sun in her life, and because Yeonja had been too mired in her own pain, she had failed to realize that Jungsoon was also nursing her own wounds.

From that day onwards, Yeonja redoubled her efforts to cook for Jungsoon and iron her clothes. She would fetch the bath water for Jungsoon, whose legs would get swollen after standing at work the whole day. Despite being only two years apart in age, they became parents to each other. Then one day Jungsoon found out she had cancer. Because she didn't want to spend her last days at the hospital, she refused chemotherapy. Her final months were spent at home, and for Yeonja the memories were still fresh in her mind.

'I miss Jungsoon eonnie. She's no longer with us,' said Yeonja, her voice calm. 'I see why Jaeha kept asking me to come here. There's something about this place that puts my heart at ease. And the petals were so pretty.'

Jieun smiled encouragingly. She had a curious feeling that she'd known Yeonja for a long time. She wanted to be there for her, to listen to her until the last knot in her heart was freed. Yeonja seemed to sink deeper into her memories.

'I do have one regret . . . When Jaeha was in high school, I was told that his father – that man – had a terminal disease. He didn't have much time left and wanted to meet with Jaeha . . . He never sent us a single won of child support, but I guess he suddenly thought of his son on his deathbed. I asked Jaeha if he wanted to meet with his father, but he refused. Nothing I said could persuade him. Once he made his decision, he stuck to it.

'Then the news came. The man had died. I thought Jaeha should at least attend the funeral – this was his father after all – so I took him there without telling him where we were going. We stood in front of the funeral home for a long time before turning back. I wondered if I should have dragged him inside even though he didn't want to go, made him see his father's funeral portrait at least . . . but at the same time, I wondered what was the point . . .'

Yeonja wasn't crying. Any tears shed for that man would be a waste.

'Sajangnim, I've shared too much, haven't I? I'm sorry. But talking about it has taken a weight off my chest. Thank you. You know, you look just like Jungsoon eonnie when she smiled. I was startled when I saw you just now. Perhaps that's why I'm talking a lot more today.'

Yeonja dabbed away her tears with a handkerchief. *Have we ever met?* Jieun wondered. Her memory was hazy. She thought she had a good memory, but a million lives were too many to remember.

'I'm happy to lend a listening ear. You seem familiar, too. It's as if we've met somewhere before.'

Yeonja was tearing up again, so Jieun poured her more tea and filled her own cup, too. It was a special brew for Yeonja, and by drinking it, Jieun was sharing her feelings. In the background, the music had stopped, but the silence was comfortable, so she let it be.

'Let me help you. Wear the t-shirt and tell me the pain you'd like to wipe away.'

Yeonja opened her eyes and turned to Jieun. She finally had enough courage to meet Jieun's gaze. Her tears had stopped, and there was a faint smile on her face.

'I know it's rude to cry in front of someone I'm meeting for the first time, but I feel much more refreshed. I haven't cried in so long.'

'It's OK. In my line of work, it'd be even more awkward if you maintained a poker face.'

The two women chuckled and their eyes met. They lifted their cups at the same time and sipped.

'I used to think that my life was the most wretched, and nobody had suffered more than me. But as life went on, I learned to carry the burden. I wasn't the only one suffering. And these days my life is the most blissful it has ever been. My heart is at ease. Seeing the gorgeous sunsets on my evening bus rides moves me. And in the mornings, when I'm the only passenger, it feels like I'm on a little holiday in my private vehicle. Sajangnim, have you tried riding the bus?'

'Hmm? I can walk home from the laundry and there's no reason for me to go anywhere.'

'Find an excuse, then. Try hopping on a bus to the city centre. The view is amazing in the day. You can people-watch through the big windows.'

Jieun nodded. *A bus holiday* . . . One more thing to add to her bucket list in this life.

'Happiness is all around us. Imagine jolting awake thinking that you're running late, only to realize it's the weekend. You fall back into bed and doze off happily. Sleeping in never felt sweeter. I enjoy the little things like this in life now,' said Yeonja. 'True, there were many moments when I wished I didn't have to suffer, but it's those times that make me appreciate how happy I am today. I have nothing to erase. The past made me who I am today, and it gave me Jaeha.'

'I see . . .'

Jieun blinked back her surprise. The swirl of petals on standby also paused, quivering in mid-air. *She may look delicate, but she's the strongest of us all.* How could she possibly want to hold on to the pain? A quiet ringing reverberated in Jieun's heart, undulating as it rose to a crescendo. Yeonja's words rang beautifully like music.

'I'm studying at an online university now, taking classes in counselling psychology. Because of my life experiences, I can better empathize with what others are going through. Life's strange, isn't it? Back then, I desperately wished to end it all. The pain was cutting me up. I craved death. But now, all these heartaches are part of me. Without them, I wouldn't be the person I am.

'I'm going to enrol in the Department of Food and Nutrition next. Food is the source of life. A warm, full stomach makes us stronger. My dream is to open a restaurant selling food for the soul. Make a living and learn new things – that's how I'll spend the rest of my life.'

Yeonja pulled on the t-shirt that she'd been hugging. Jieun was a little alarmed. *Why is she putting it on when she doesn't want to erase anything? Does she have some bigger pain that I failed to notice?*

When Yeonja stood up, her gaze was steady.

'I don't dislike my life. It used to be me brainwashing myself to like it because it'd be so pathetic not to. But once I started to be more positive, life truly began to feel beautiful. Since my son wants to present me with this experience, I'll accept it gracefully. Please don't erase anything. Just help me smooth out the creases and make the memories less painful to recall.'

The petals turned merry cartwheels in mid-air. Jieun smiled as the petals swirling by Yeonja's feet danced in rhythm as if applauding her, then led her enthusiastically upstairs to the ironing corner. Yeonja's eyes widened in surprise.

'Omo! Goodness gracious! How pretty you all are. What an extraordinary day this is!'

She was glad to be alive. She lived because she was born, because she was given life. She lived because she couldn't die. Little by little, she started to enjoy living each day and being alive felt like a blessing. It took Yeonja a long time to realize that the making of a happy life was not at the mercy of others, but where our hearts led. Perhaps her journey long and far through a dark tunnel was to allow her to realize that it takes practice to reach happiness.

As long as we're alive, all stains are beautiful. Knowing that life is short, that we exist in the moment, is something worth being grateful for. Stirring out of her reverie, Yeonja watched from behind as Jieun ironed the t-shirt with care. *If Jungsoon eonnie had had a daughter, she'd be just as pretty . . .*

'Here, it's perfectly pressed. But you do know, right, that once you put it back on, the wrinkles are going to come back?'

'Of course. Whether it's something ugly like wrinkles or something beautiful, they're all a part of my life. The t-shirt feels warm and toasty. Thank you.'

As she reached for the t-shirt, she gave Jieun's hand a gentle squeeze. The warmth spread, reaching all the way to their hearts, enveloping them in comfort. Yeonja had never felt more at peace.

'Ms Yeonja! I'm off work! Are you there?'

The front door opened and Jaeha's bubbly voice carried up the stairs. Jieun and Yeonja chuckled at the same time. The ribbon of petals wrapped around them, and in a swirl they dropped at the entrance in front of Jaeha. Having been staring up towards the first floor, he leapt back in surprise.

'Damn. Ms Yeonja, you're already used to riding the petals? That's fast. Did you make my favourite soy-braised quail eggs? I brought rice. Let's have dinner. Sajangnim, come join us. Ms Yeonja's side dishes are the best!'

Jaeha's energy filled the space and the three of them smiled. Nothing beat the warmth of great company. Outside, it was a chilly autumn evening, but inside, it was cosy and snug.

'Sajangnim, the flowers on your dress are purple today.'

'Really? They look red as usual to me.'

'Eh? You're right. But I thought I saw a flash of purple . . . Ms Yeonja loves flowers, too. I think that's why I keep noticing your dress,' Jaeha laughed.

Rat-tat-tat.

Someone was knocking on the door. Who could it be? She wasn't expecting anyone.

Jieun got up.

'Is this the Marigold Mind Laundry? You have a parcel from a Lee Yeonhee.'

In the deliveryman's hand was a small package; he held out a slip for signature. The world was becoming a better place. In just a day, Yeonhee's parcel had reached the seaside village. Jieun scribbled her signature and was about to return the slip when her eyes landed on the man's wrists. Strapped on his left wrist was a digital watch with a large display showing the time down to the second, and on his right was a smartwatch. He took the slip, gave a short bow, and turned to record the delivery time before pressing down his cap and disappearing into the dark back streets.

A moment later, Jieun felt someone watching her from the dark.

'Who's that? Is someone there?'

But all was quiet. Cocking her head to the side, she closed the door behind her and walked towards the alleyway. She peered into it for a second before looking up to the sky and taking a deep breath. The cold air, carrying with it the smell of the sea and autumn leaves, filled her lungs. In the background, the wind rustled, stirring up the fallen leaves. The seasons were always faithful. Summer had made a quiet exit, and autumn had taken its place.

'Oh, was that Uncle Yeonghui delivering a package? What are you doing out here alone? Come on, let's eat before the food gets cold!' Jaeha had come out to find her and was now tugging at Jieun's elbow.

'Uncle Yeonghui?'

'Yeah, he's been around in the neighbourhood for a long time. I think his name is Kim Yeonghui? He doesn't talk about his past, though – where he came from, what he used to do – but he's our go-to person for delivery. He helps the elderly grannies living on the hill to carry their stuff home, and if you ask him to move bulky items, he's happy to do it. We all call him Uncle Yeonghui.'

'He sounds like a great person. Let's go back inside.'

'It's time to eat. That's right. Eat to live and live to eat. And like Yeonja said, take the bus and go sightseeing. Enjoy life.'

Enjoy life. The corners of her lips lifted slightly.

That sounds good.

Yeonja and Jaeha left after dinner. Jieun saw them off at the door, and in her heart she hoped that they would find peace. She watched them walk hand in hand, disappearing into the distance. The mind laundry had been born out of her desire to release herself from her own fate. She'd taken it as a given that everyone would want to wash themselves clean of stains, but as she met people like Yeonja, who'd asked for a little ironing instead, Jieun started to question her assumption. What exactly were feelings?

They were neither visible nor tangible, yet they held so much power. Our emotions can spur us to start something new, to resolve issues, or even to put an end to things. Sometimes flowers bloom in our hearts, other times feelings can cause us to wallow in misery. Perhaps the start and end to everything is these unfathomable things called *feelings*.

Her thoughts continued to swirl as she locked the door and walked up to the snack shop, package in hand. *Have I ever considered my own feelings carefully?* Despite having lived a million lives, she had never taken the time to look into her own heart. Nor had she given much thought to her emotions.

Feelings were like flowers. You could tend to them, let them bask in the sunlight, and they might wilt, bloom, begin to rot, give off smells, attract insects. But later, new leaves might sprout, along with a fresh bud.

Feelings seemed to be at once beautiful and sad. Why couldn't they be beautiful without being sad? But what did it even mean, to be *beautiful*? We're taught that sadness and pain aren't beautiful, while happiness and joy are. But what if the opposite were true? Imagine if people started to realize that beauty lies in pain and sadness; would the way we view the world crumble? Maybe that's why it's a hidden secret. Perhaps.

Even after such a long life, there were still many things she didn't know.

★

'Ajumma, you haven't gone home? I heard your knees are hurting. Yeonhee sent you these.'

'Aigoo, did she? What a lovely child. She didn't have to.'

Despite what she said, she had a smile on her face. Jieun noticed that the ajumma had been massaging her knees more often than usual. She set the package on the red table, still as sticky as ever with the grease stains.

'Ajumma. Can't these stains be washed off?' Jieun asked, tapping a finger on the table.

The ajumma set down the spring onions she was chopping and grabbed a rag to wipe the table.

'They've been there for a long time, so it's hard to get them out. What can I do? It's still like this, no matter how much I wipe. But it's fine, only people who don't mind come in anyway.'

'Ajumma, that's why most people order takeaway. If you want people to eat in, the tables have to be clean. How about I buy you new ones?'

'Aigoo, it's fine,' she said, waving away the offer with the spring onions in her hand. 'I wouldn't be able to handle more customers on my own anyway. So what if I could earn more money? I'm getting by just fine.'

New tables would indeed look out of place. The nickel-silver pots and faded plastic plates, together with the old red tables, somehow added to the shop's charm. The ajumma cleared away the ingredients and opened the box. Inside were bottles of medicine. Looking at the ajumma massage her knees out of habit, Jieun suddenly felt an ache in her own. That was strange. Was she experiencing the ajumma's pain in her own body, the same way she shared people's feelings?

'Would taking this help to relieve the pain?' Jieun said as she stared at the bottles. 'My knees are aching, too. Have I lived too long?'

'Try this, then. Take care of your body while you're young. Or else you'll have a rough time when you're my age. Here, take one.'

'It's fine. You have it. I'll get Yeonhee to send me some.'

'Aigoo, just take this and ask her to get you more later.'

'Oh . . . all right, then.'

Pretending that she couldn't reject the offer, Jieun took the proffered bottle. It was time to go back. She needed to close up shop for the day. Ever since she'd realized that the ajumma would wait for her to wind down for the day before winding down herself, Jieun stopped staying until the small hours of the morning.

At first, Jieun couldn't quite understand the point of the ajumma sitting in her empty shop, dozing off and waiting, but after spending a few seasons together, she realized how comforting it was to see the lights on inside the snack shop. On days when the ajumma closed early for her doctor's appointments, Jieun found herself feeling listless and her footsteps dragging. Humans are such peculiar creatures. We want to keep an appropriate distance, yet we also wish people to be sufficiently close by.

Jieun picked up a black plastic bag. The ajumma always prepared two rolls of kimbap for her breakfast the next morning. At the door, she turned around, holding the medicine bottle in one hand and the kimbap in the other.

'Ajumma. Don't fall sick. Take good care of yourself and live for a long time. Don't scrimp on doctor's fees. If you don't have enough, I'll help you – take it as payment for the kimbap.'

'Sure, sure. That's very reassuring. But it's just the usual aches of an old woman – no need to fuss. At this age, all I can do is to soothe the pains and ailments and live out the rest of my days. Come on, time to go. You must be tired after hosting Yeonja at the laundry. You've worked hard today, too.'

Sending Jieun on her way, the ajumma yawned. It was also time for her to close up for the night.

Through the shop's glass doors, the ajumma watched with satisfaction as Jieun walked away. She used to be so thin and listless that it wouldn't have been a surprise if she'd crumbled away at any moment. But it seemed like she was slowly finding herself again. Jieun hadn't seemed to realize that the ingredients that went into the two rolls of kimbap were different every day. But all the same, she always seemed to finish her food. That was good enough.

The petals hadn't followed Jieun back to the laundry. The ajumma glanced at them as if they were humans, and gave one of them a little tap with her finger.

'You pretty little ones, don't worry. There's a right time for everything. Good things will come soon. As long as you believe in that, you'll be fine. So you all should return to where you belong.'

The petals turned cartwheels at her words before disappearing. On a night when the air was filled with care and warmth, a restful sleep came easily. The moonlight cast a gentle glow on the back streets. Such a night felt more radiant than the day. What was in the dark didn't have to be darkness, what was in the light didn't have to be light. Light could be found in the darkness, just as darkness could be found in the light.

It was one such gentle night.

Chapter VIII

BEATING HEARTS

The wind blew, spreading news of the mind laundry atop the hill. With high school students keen to erase the pain of failed exams, Jieun was kept busy with a stream of visitors coming in with stains of varying shapes and sizes. In the day, she brewed the healing tea, listened to their stories and soothed the hurt in their hearts. In the evenings, she released the petals into the sunset.

It was only on Friday nights, when she usually closed early to prepare for the following week, that the laundry settled back into its quiet hum. The lights on the sign were switched off and the petals sent on their way, leaving behind a trail of perfume as they cartwheeled towards the sea. Ever since she'd resolved to make the best of the powers bestowed on her, life had become more fulfilling. Life, death. Both were monosyllabic words, but the weight they carried couldn't be more opposite. Having made up her mind to seek death, Jieun was living each day to the fullest.

Jaeha and Yeonhee dropped by regularly in the evenings. Sometimes Hae-in would join them, and they'd have dinner together, chatting and listening to music. Hae-in was busy preparing for his solo photography exhibit. Yeonhee, too, had good news. Having been selected as a top employee for ten years in a row, she'd been promoted to training manager for frontline staff at the headquarters.

There was something comforting about sharing life updates with one another. *But do I deserve to feel this way?* At the slightest hint of pleasure and satisfaction, Jieun would be consumed by an intense guilt. A mixture of longing and regret washed over her as she mechanically folded the t-shirts and placed them neatly in the drawer.

'Need any help?'

It was late afternoon when Hae-in appeared at the door, carrying a box of cookies he'd bought along the way. He came up to Jieun and picked up a t-shirt. It smelled like sunshine, and something else pleasant.

What a clean and lovely smell. Makes me feel happy, just like Jieun-ssi.

'What?'

'Huh? Did I say something?'

'You said, *What a clean and lovely smell. Makes me happy, just like Jieun-ssi.*'

'. . . Ah . . .'

Hae-in's ears blushed a deep crimson. He hadn't realized he'd said *that* aloud.

Oh no.

'Why *oh no*? It's true, I am clean, lovely and make people happy.'

'Um. I don't know why I'm speaking my thoughts aloud. I'm just not usually much of a talker . . .'

Jieun burst out laughing. *What an earnest guy*, she thought.

'Maybe you just enjoy chatting with me. Anyway, are you free right now?'

'Yes, of course!'

'Help me by folding these while I go upstairs to tidy up. Thank you!'

Jieun pressed a pile of t-shirts into Hae-in's arms, a hint of mischief in her eyes as she turned to go. The swirl of petals swooped in, twirling in circles around them.

Thump, thump, thump.

Oh, my heart! Why is it beating so loudly? Unknowingly, they each raised a palm to their chest, feeling their heartbeats at the same time.

'An extra pair of hands makes so much difference. I was a little tired today, so I really appreciate that. And if you're not in a rush, would you help me hang the laundry, too?'

'Of course! Anything else you need?'

The petals, which were resting by their feet, rustled up. Like the chariots in Emily Dickinson's poems, it was as if both of them were riding on a flower carriage, lovingly carried by the swirling petals. How long does it take to fall in love? And was that her heart skipping a beat? Jieun was flustered at the strange feeling bubbling in her. But it felt good.

'These petals are pretty.'

'Yeah. They've been keeping me company so I don't feel lonely.'

'Ah, I should thank them, then.'

'The sun is still strong in the afternoon. It's the perfect day to hang laundry.'

Jieun handed Hae-in a shirt from the basket. He shook it hard, twice, and spread it out on the clothes line. Behind them, the sunlight was glittering.

Hae-in stole a glance at Jieun. With her back to the sun, it was as if she was glowing. *How I wish this moment could last forever.* Wait, was there any other time he'd felt this way? The sadness in his heart was always whipping time to go faster. Instead of wanting more out of life, he'd long resigned himself to accepting whatever fate doled out to him. But right now, a breeze was tickling his heart. If ever there was a moment in life he'd want to hold on to, he thought this was it.

'Isn't this so beautiful? A sea of white fluttering in the wind on the rooftop.'

'Indeed. I should've brought my camera.'

'Capture it with your eyes and keep it in your heart. True beauty can't be preserved within a frame. Pictures are lovely, but if it's a moment to be cherished forever, you won't want to miss anything. Be present – wholly, unreservedly – and remember it with your heart.'

Hae-in nodded. They turned to stand shoulder to shoulder and watched the sun dip beyond the horizon. Behind them, the clothes danced in the wind. This was it. The beautiful moment he wanted to cherish forever.

Chapter IX

UNCLE YEONGHUI

R*AT-TAT-TAT.*

'Sajangnim. You've got a package.'

Must be the supplements from Yeonhee, Jieun thought as she quickly closed the drawer and headed towards the door, the patterns on her dress swaying.

When she returned the signed slip to Uncle Yeonghui, Jieun's gaze landed on his wrists. Like the previous time, he was wearing two watches and checking the time on the digital one before recording it.

But today, he didn't leave immediately. He stood there, looking as though he had something to say. There was an air of resolve in the way he solemnly took off his cap and carried it under his arm. There were six pockets on his vest, but he reached past them into the inner lining and pulled out a piece of paper folded into quarters. The edges were fraying and the corners dog-eared. He held it out to Jieun, keeping his eyes low.

'I-I picked this up by chance and have been keeping it with me. Am I at the right place?'

We remove stains from the heart and mind,
and erase your painful memories.

If it makes you happier,
we can also iron out any creases,
and get rid of unwanted blotches.

We remove all types of stains.
Welcome to the Marigold Mind Laundry.

Yours sincerely,
The Owner

Her eyes tracked the words and she nodded. The leaflet, barely held together by tape, looked as though it must have been folded and unfolded countless times. *What made him keep the paper so close to his heart?* It must have been fate that there was one serving of tea left. She was still thinking about having it herself. *But it looks like I've found the person who needs it more tonight.*

'Yes, I made these on our opening day. I haven't seen one for a while, though. Are we your last stop today? If so, come in and have a cup of tea.'

'Oh . . . But I'm all sweaty right now. The smell . . .'

'No worries. We're a laundry – that can be solved in a jiffy. Come in.'

Yeonghui scratched his head, looking hesitant. It was clear from his expression that something was holding him back. Jieun pushed the door wide open and gestured for him to follow. The invitation was given; it was now up to him to muster the courage. She took a deep breath and glanced up in the direction of the sea. At her signal, the petals whooshed in with the wind and orbited the laundry. Even at this magical sight, Yeonghui remained oddly unmoved. Because it wasn't his first time seeing the petals.

That first night, Yeonghui had also been here, watching. He'd been in his van, catching a catnap after a full day of deliveries. Stirring awake, he'd been greeted by an unfamiliar sight unfolding in front of him. He'd rubbed his eyes to make sure he wasn't hallucinating – a building had just manifested itself from nowhere! Moments later, he saw Jaeha and Yeonhee walking in.

He'd pocketed one of the leaflets that had floated down on to his van window, carrying it with him wherever he went. Over the passing seasons, he quietly observed Jieun and her visitors. A stranger to the village claiming to erase painful memories? No way. He wasn't a brave man, but if this laundry was doing something shady under the guise of kindness, he would have no qualms about rushing in and closing it down. Every time he passed by the laundry on the way to a delivery, he made sure to log his observations.

The seasons waxed and waned, but all he noticed was that visitors would leave with a hint of a smile on their faces. While there were some tears and an occasional sigh, he could still tell that there was an aura of peace around them.

It was then that he turned his attention to the owner of the laundry: the woman who cried on the rooftop every evening. Somehow her tears reminded him of petals, and silently he observed what she was up to. She didn't seem like the type to hurt anyone.

Biting down hard on his lip, Yeonghui came to a decision.

'If there was ever any bit of luck landing in my life, it's right now,' he murmured, scraping the mud from his shoes on the edge of the wooden steps. He gripped his cap tightly and glanced at his watch. 7:07 p.m. And . . .

'Seven-o-eight.'

Just then, droplets of water started to pelt his watch display. It was raining.

He ran up the seven steps and stood under the eaves. For him, opening doors was a herculean task. Part of the reason he became a deliveryman was because he'd never have to open a door – either the door would be opened for him, or he could simply leave the parcels by the entrance. Holding the doorknob and pulling – or pushing – open the door might sound trivial, but for some people, including him, it required resolve.

Keeping his gaze fixed on the leaves rustling with the weight of the raindrops, he gave a little nod to steel himself. With a glance at his watch – it was 7:11 p.m. – he stepped inside. Three minutes was all it took to cook the perfect ramyeon, but the past three minutes felt like a compression of three decades of his life. The clock in his heart, which had paused for the longest time, was starting again. *Tick tock, tick tock.*

Inside him, something was pounding. Was it his heart, or the clock?

At five minutes to nine, Yeonghui stood at the door with his school bag. He chewed his nails nervously, his eyes fixed on his watch. Seconds, then minutes passed. As the dial turned to nine o'clock sharp, he had no choice but to push open the door and leave for school. If only he didn't have to. He wouldn't mind leaving the door forever shut.

'Kim Yeonghui! Look at the time now. Late again! Go to the corner and put your hands above your head!'

Yeonghui's uniform was soaked in sweat. A habitual late-comer, he was used to the punishments from the discipline master hollering at him now – running laps of the field with hands raised or cleaning the toilets. But in fact his house was only ten minutes away on foot, where he lived with his university professor father, lawyer mother and his older brother, Yeongsu, who was every bit the model student.

Everyone else at home was perpetually busy, so in their family it was of the utmost importance that the day's schedule was adhered to, right down to the second. Yeonghui, on the other hand, would rather wait for the rest of them to leave before slowly munching on the two remaining sandwiches on the dining table.

The part-time housekeeper who came every day also ran like clockwork. She arrived at their doorstep on the dot of ten, and until two in the afternoon she would clean, do the laundry and make the side dishes. After methodically getting through the day's work, she would, at exactly ten past two, leave the house. This was when Yeonghui would time his escape back home.

'Who in the neighbourhood doesn't know of your brilliant brother? You have a professor as a father and your mother is a lawyer. How is it that you're so tardy? Learn from your brother – just being half of him would be good enough! Aigoo.' The discipline master clucked his tongue in disapproval. 'OK, off you go.'

Yeonghui's face was an inscrutable blank as he held his hands above his head. Everyone knew his famous older brother, who had graduated from the same school. Next to Yeonghui, hands above their heads, the other latecomers stared daggers at him. Feeling the unspoken pressure, Yeonghui spoke up.

'I . . . Sir. I'll help with the cleaning of the toilets.'

'Who said anything about cleaning toilets? Shoo, go back to class. And hey, you two over there! Go clean the toilets on the ground floor! Rascals, this'll teach you not to be late!'

It looked like the discipline master was reluctant to punish Yeonghui today for fear that it would reach the ears of his parents, who chaired the School Development Committee. *I'd rather they found out*, Yeonghui thought as he shuffled to his classroom on the first floor. He peered through the crack of the door. First period had already started. He would have to open the door. Yeonghui squeezed his eyes shut and pushed.

Inside the classroom, the atmosphere was frigid. He bowed his head a fraction at the teacher, who was talking, and quickly slid into his seat. This was it – the start. *Please, please, please.*

Until the class bell rang, the second and minute hands on the wall clock seemed to tick obscenely loudly, like his heart. Anxiety gripped him.

Ding dong deng dong.

At the bell, the teacher collected her books and left. The pounding clock fell silent. Yeonghui's eyes were tightly shut, but he could sense them approaching.

'Oi. Didn't I tell you to come early and clean our desks? Do I look like I'm joking?'

Yeonghui kept his head bowed and his eyes screwed tight. He tightened his grip on his bag. *Go, run. Now!* he screamed to himself. The next moment, something sloshed down from above his head. Instantly, his senses were overpowered by a rancid smell. *At least it's white today.*

'Oops. My hands slipped. *SOR-RI*,' a drawling voice said. 'Hey, drink this.'

Jinsu, who'd emptied half the packet of spoilt milk over him, forced his mouth open and poured in the remainder.

'N-no, st-sto . . .' he spluttered and coughed.

'What? Stop? Did you just order me to *stop*? Dumbass. Drag him out.'

'S-sorry. I-it's my fault.'

'Oho? Well, if you're sorry, then don't do it in the first place? What? You wanna say something? Snitch to your parents, for all I care.'

Even as Yeonghui was dragged away, sobbing and blubbering, nobody in the class tried to stop anything. Jinsu was infamous at school, and no one could beat him in a fight. Screaming,

Yeonghui threw desperate looks at his classmates, but they avoided his eyes. Someone had once called the form teacher over, but Jinsu beat that kid up so badly everyone was scared. Resigned to his fate, Yeonghui closed his eyes. Time would pass. Things would be fine again. As long as he could make it through till the next bell, the pain, the torment would come to an end. *But would there ever be an end?*

Ding dong deng dong. Ding dong deng dong.

The bell for the next period rang. Jinsu and his gang dropped him and returned to their seats.

The wall clock, which had fallen silent, started pounding again. In life, there were times when minutes stretched longer than eternity. Like right now. And in fifty minutes, when the next period ended, another eternity would await him. To hide the fact that he'd been beaten up, Yeonghui propped up his textbook on the desk and buried his head behind it. His eyes darted between the clock and the door. *I want to escape.* If only he could push open the door before the next break, before the gang closed in on him again. Open the door and run out – that was all he wanted to do. Yet nothing could have been more impossible.

'What a sudden downpour. The weather forecast didn't mention any rain. You must be drenched. Here, dry yourself with this towel.'

Inside the laundry, Yeonghui stayed by the door with his eyes closed. Jieun could tell from his expression that he was trapped in the agony of his past. Sometimes what her visitors really needed was not the power of her magic, but some warmth. Yeonghui was one of those. If he would let her, she wanted to give his heart a close hug. The petals, as though reading Jieun's mind, twirled out from her dress. Hearing their whoosh, Yeonghui opened his eyes and his furrowed brows gradually relaxed. Out of habit, he checked the time before glancing at the petals and then back to Jieun.

He nodded in thanks and dried himself. 'Sorry to trouble you, and thank you.'

When the petals brought him a white t-shirt, he took it, shaking his head to rid himself of the memories that had surfaced. Memories from thirty years ago. Why were they still seared in his mind? To escape the misery, he'd uprooted himself and settled down far away in this village. Decades had passed since then, but the torment still haunted him. Just as a fleeting memory can fuel us to keep going in life, there are times our past clings on, torturing our hearts.

'Take a seat and have some tea. There's just enough for one. It must be meant for you,' said Jieun as she filled a mug, deliberately choosing an unassuming vessel to make him feel at ease.

He must have been thirsty. In a single breath, he gulped down the lukewarm tea. No words could truly comfort someone who was suffering on the inside, so Jieun was glad that she was bestowed with the power to make healing tea. *Wait.* She caught a whiff of something. The smell of autumn, like fallen leaves on the ground. Something stirred in her memories. What was it?

As if he'd read her mind, Yeonghui spoke up. 'I have something to confess. I've been observing the laundry for a while. Not out of malice, of course. But after I witnessed something so unbelievable, I was afraid that strange things might start to happen in the neighbourhood.'

He was noticeably less guarded; the healing tea must have taken effect. As if on cue, the petals stopped swirling and returned to her dress.

'I did feel like I was being watched. And each time, I smelled autumn leaves. So that was you. I didn't sense any ill feelings, so I waited. I knew that the person would eventually show themselves. Our laundry is quite an interesting place, isn't it?'

Jieun's lips were turned up in a slight smile, playfulness twinkling in her eyes. These days, with more people in her life, she had become a lot chattier. She even attempted to crack the odd joke, although nobody could ever quite tell if it was supposed to be one.

'Oh . . . you knew. If I made you uncomfortable, I'd like to apologize.'

'Apology accepted. But no, it's fine.'

'In that case, could I ask for your help to erase an old stain on my heart? It's been there for a long, long time.'

'I haven't had any problems so far. Wear the t-shirt and go up to the laundry room. Close your eyes, think back to the memories you wish to wipe away, and they'll spread as stains on the t-shirt. Once I wash the shirt, the spots will be gone. You already have an idea how this works, right?'

'Yes. And once the shirt is washed, I'll have to hang it on the clothes line on the rooftop, right? Can I ask a question?'

'Ask away.'

'When the t-shirts are dry, where do they go? Will they also become petals?'

The questions seemed to burst out of him. He usually avoided talking but, strangely, something akin to courage was welling up in him right now.

'You're holding a t-shirt that has been washed and dried. Petals won't appear out of it. The petals are the hurt and pain freed from stains, and every evening I release them to the sunset. They'll burn to become light, and at night they'll become stars.'

'Sounds impossible. How can pain ever become flowers and light?'

'The mind laundry is where the impossible becomes possible.'

'Not my pain. That'll never become petals.'

'You may think so. We all believe our wounds to be the biggest, the most painful. So overwhelming that we can't seem to muster the courage to do anything – apply cream or seek treatment – and all we can do is hide the pain deep down in our hearts. At least the wounds on our skin crust into scabs, but the ones in our hearts remain raw. Just as a cut gets worse if we touch it, the same goes for the pain in our hearts.'

'That's right. It hurts so much.'

Yeonghui shrugged out of his vest and draped it over the chair. He put the t-shirt on and checked his watch. 8:55 p.m. His eyes widened in shock. How had the time passed so quickly?

'Sajangnim, am I taking up too much of your time?'

'Yes, you've been here for a while – but it's no time at all compared to the pain you've been carrying. Don't worry.'

Jieun, who was smiling with her arms crossed, had read his mind. At Yeonghui's feet, the petals circled enthusiastically for a moment before flapping like butterflies on to the floor. *Follow us*, they seemed to be saying. Yeonghui took a step forward.

His footsteps were sturdy and firm, as if he were putting the weight of his entire life into them. All he had done was drink tea and share a little about himself. How had he suddenly gained the courage to take the first step forward? He took a deep breath and walked towards the stairs. Slowly, the stains spread on to his t-shirt.

It was 9:05 p.m.

Yeonghui walked through the door that opened for him on its own and stepped inside. *How sunny it feels*. It made no sense; it was night-time, and they were indoors. But he swore he could feel the sun on his skin.

He had spent a lot of time observing the laundry from the outside. Yet, inside, it felt so much warmer and cosier than he'd imagined. Indeed, seeing something from the outside was completely different from experiencing it himself. Most of the time we choose what we want to see, hear and feel. Just like how we only ever show a certain side of ourselves and share only what we're comfortable with.

Through the window, the downpour showed no signs of abating.

'The weather forecast this morning did mention the possibility of rain – but only a thirty per cent probability. That's why I didn't think much of it when I left home. Can't believe it's really pouring,' said Yeonghui.

'I guess you check the weather every day?'

'Yeah. My job is mostly outdoors, after all. Wouldn't it be nice if we could forecast the weather in our lives, too? Like how it'll be wet for the next couple of days, but the sun will return the following week. Or that it'll be cloudy but remain dry. If only it were possible to know ahead of time that once we've battled through the bout of bad weather, we can look forward to enjoying perfect skies for a while.'

'That would be lovely.'

Looking a little wistful, Yeonghui stared out the window. A part in his chest grew hot and constricted. As if his heart were burning, a fire cartwheeling within him. He was used to swallowing and suppressing the burning heat, but today the fire was releasing as he spoke. If words had colour, his would be flaming red today.

Jieun could sense the raging fire in his heart, but she kept quiet.

Yeonghui sat down at the table behind Jieun, who was watching the washing machine.

'Sometimes living is more difficult than dying,' he said.

Jieun turned around. *That's right. Life is much tougher.* There's a saying: Live with the courage of facing death. But the living cannot have experienced death, so would anyone really know how much courage is required to die? Just how much more resilient do we have to become in order to live, and to live happily? Jieun deeply empathized with the pain that Yeonghui had struggled with for decades. Sometimes all it takes is a simple nod and a knowing look for our feelings and thoughts to reverberate, to spread further than any words can. Yeonghui felt a rush of warmth to his heart.

'That's right. Nobody knows for sure – how much more effort do we have to put in, how much harder must we try? Because life's impossible to predict, that's why we feel overwhelmed. I do, too.'

'But you seem to have everything . . . Even you feel this way?'

'Do I look like I have everything?'

'Yes.'

'Well, thanks for seeing me in such a positive light. Perhaps I do. I might have everything, or maybe nothing at all. But does life become blissful just because of what we own?'

'I . . . I don't know.'

'The strength to live is not linked to how much or little we possess. Unless we're talking about the power to bounce back from sadness or to praise ourselves for having made it through a day.'

'If only there were magical powers to grant us such strength.'

'Oh! Why didn't I think of that! Should I come up with something?' Jieun's hand flew to her mouth in exaggerated revelation. At her playful look, the last of Yeonghui's anxiety evaporated. A stain spread and darkened on his shirt.

He stared down at the dark patches on the once pristine shirt.

'I have an older brother, Yeongsu. My parents apparently wanted a daughter next, and they'd already decided her name – Yeonghui. From the moment I was born, I couldn't meet their expectations. Mother, Father and Yeongsu were brilliant; I was the only loser in the family. My grades were terrible, not to mention how I was always ostracized in school. I didn't even dare to tell my family about the bullying. I was scared of disappointing my parents. They'd probably be ashamed of me because I was nothing like my brother. Every day was a struggle . . .'

His sadness seemed to cut too deep for tears to flow. Yeonghui swallowed the dry, painful lump in his throat and continued calmly.

'I should've hung in there until I finished high school, but it was too much to bear. My parents were against me dropping out. But if I'd stayed on, I thought I might just kill all those bastards.

'So I quit. The day I graduated high school as a private candidate, a scene I'd read in a book suddenly crossed my mind. Someone went to the train station on the spur of the moment and said, "One ticket for the next train, please." I had no idea what got into me . . . but I immediately packed my bags and did the same. That was how I ended up here, in Marigold.

'It gave me peace of mind to be assured that nobody knew me here. I didn't have to go to school; my tormentors were far away. My parents insisted that I come home and even sent someone to fetch me, but I refused.'

Jieun waved her hand and the lights dimmed. Grateful to have someone pay attention to his story, Yeonghui continued.

'For about half a year, all I did was walk along the shore and around the village. I would head out first thing in the morning, and at sunset I'd take a short break before carrying on. Naturally, I became very familiar with the streets and addresses. Then, one day, I saw a hiring notice for a deliveryman. That was how I ended up in this job.'

'Isn't it tough work?'

'Physically, yes. But when people thank me for my help, I feel like a useful person for a change. Back then, I was a kid who was bullied at school, and at home I was the second child who'd never match up to my brother . . .' His voice faltered.

'So, I continued to do deliveries, surviving day by day right up to now. And after all these years, here I am, meeting you.'

'What is the stain you wish to wipe away?'

'I've been mulling it over for a long time. Being seen as helpful here makes me feel like I've become a better person. But when I think about it, why is it that I need acknowledgement? It's not my fault that I'm not as brilliant as the rest of my family . . . Even when I was being bullied, I didn't have the courage to stand up for myself. I simply thought I deserved it for being a loser. For not being good enough. I want to wipe away the part of me that thinks everything is my fault, that I'm only at peace if I'm being validated by others, and the obsession I have with time because of my family.'

'So that's why you're always looking at your watch . . . It must've been hard for you.'

There was a moment of silence.

'Am I supposed to take off the shirt now and put it in the washing machine? Is that all?'

Now that he'd let out what he'd kept bottled up for such a long time, Yeonghui looked a lot more relaxed as he took off the t-shirt and gave it a good shake. With a flick of Jieun's right wrist the red petals glowed, and she lifted the t-shirt out of his hands and into the washing machine. The petals followed behind, joining the wash. If there was ever going to be a time when his feelings could be removed and washed clean, this was it. Yeonghui stared open-mouthed at the sight. Jieun's voice was low.

'You've been through a lot – in the past, and today, too. When tomorrow comes, don't keep suffering; learn to smile a little more. And the day after tomorrow, stop bottling up your emotions. Forcing yourself to endure is a way of life, but as time passes the only memories you'll have are of you struggling.'

It felt as if a warm blanket were being laid on his weary heart. It was true that his most vivid memories to date were still of the times he'd suffered. Yeonghui nodded and closed his eyes. As the washing machine spun, his feelings swirled in his heart, and calm spread over him.

The watches on his wrists were beginning to feel strangely uncomfortable. Now that he thought about it, he hadn't checked the time since coming into the laundry room. He adjusted the watch on his left wrist and massaged away the fatigue. For a moment, he stared at it. Then, he reached out to unclasp it and stuff it into his pocket. On the empty wrist was a tan line. He rubbed at it. Would it fade? Time would help, hopefully.

Pretending that she hadn't noticed, Jieun started to draw circles in the air. As her finger went round and round, they watched the petals spiral.

'I may not be as smart as my parents or my brother, but I wanted to do my best in life. I didn't want to waste a single minute, a single second, so I went everywhere with two watches. If one of them stopped working, I'd still have a backup, so I'd always be on the dot at my job. I was never late for deliveries, and whatever free time I had I'd use to help residents in the neighbourhood. It never occurred to me that wearing two watches is suffocating. But strangely, right now, I feel it is.'

Yeonghui gripped his wrist from beneath, as if putting on a watch upside down. While Jieun was considering her reply, the petals curled around his wrist. The tickling sensation made him laugh. The next moment they had glided away, and the tan line vanished. Yeonghui stared in shock. Jieun gave him a smile.

'Have you heard? If memories were made of a circle of ten, then a single good memory could blanket over the other nine bad ones. That's why it's important to make more good memories, one at a time. Let the unhappy memories sink to the bottom, and cover them with new, beautiful memories. I hope the events today can overlay the rest of the unhappy memories, like a big, warm blanket.'

The washing machine, spinning circles of red, had stopped. The door clicked open, and a whoosh of petals swirled out and carried the wet shirt towards him. It was pristine. Yeonghui broke into a toothy grin. He was liberated. *Now I know why I ended up at this neighbourhood. It's all for today.*

Shoulders trembling, he buried his face in the shirt. Jieun quietly slipped out of the laundry room, giving him space and time to feel sad about the lingering sorrow.

Today it's a little cloudy in your heart, but soon it'll clear up to be a good day for outdoor activities.

Perhaps she should prepare the weather forecast for Uncle Yeonghui, at least for the next few weeks, Jieun thought as she went back downstairs. On a piece of memo paper, she wrote the weather forecast for the next day, and slipped it inside his vest pocket. Sometimes it doesn't take much to create magic.

To release the magic in life, we need to muster the courage to open the closed door in our heart. Sometimes, no matter how hard we seem to push, pull or knock at it, the door might remain locked. Or we might have lost the key.

'But perhaps the key has always been in our pocket,' Jieun spoke quietly to the petals behind her. When would we then have the courage to unlock and push open the door?

Outside, the heavy downpour had abated to a drizzle.

For the first time in a long while, Jieun woke up early. She turned on the radio and pushed open the windows to be greeted by a salty, cool breeze. It was the cusp of another season.

She inhaled deeply, humming the tune on the radio. The segment for listeners' stories – her favourite – would start soon. As the theme tune faded out, she paid attention and waited for the host to come on.

'Good morning. This is the first time I'm writing in. I'm a deliveryman, and these days I'm also writing poetry. I usually write in my van in between deliveries, and it helps me mull over life. I've battled through a long and difficult period. For decades, I carried the pain with me, but one day I got a chance to erase it – just like magic. It didn't turn my life around completely, but it made waking up every day much easier. Life used to be a never-ending struggle, but these days I feel alive. Perhaps it was indeed a life-changing experience.

'For years on end, I was trapped in a living hell. I received a lot of hurtful remarks, and my heart felt like it was being torn apart. Despite my best efforts to connect with people, I was being continually put down. Or sometimes I was the one hurting others.

'That magical experience taught me something. Be it criticisms or even insults, I don't have to accept them. The same way we reject a parcel or return it, I can say no to humiliation and bullying – whether it's how people make me feel, what they say to me, or what they used to do to me. If I don't take it, then it isn't mine. So, what I'm saying is, if someone dislikes or even hates you, don't embrace those feelings and pain. Give them back. By doing so, the pain won't become yours. It'll rebound back to the person. Don't clog your heart with negativity. Reject abuse. You have the right to do so.'

'Here we have the story sent in by Mr Kim Yeonghui. On this gorgeous morning, you're tuning in to *My Resolve for a Beautiful Day.* Well said, Mr Kim. I will be practising how to give back and reject the pain people try to inflict on me. As for the magic of the heart, I'd love to experience it, too. Our next song is Michael Jackson's "You Are Not Alone". Indeed, you aren't alone because you're having a lovely morning with us on the radio.'

'Oh! Is that Uncle Yeonghui?'

He did look a lot more at ease after that day, Jieun thought, as the song played. *But wow, to think that he sent in his story to the radio . . .*

On the sofa, Jieun rested her head on her raised knees. She hummed along, enjoying being reminded that she was not alone. The radio kept her company. Whenever they played her favourite songs, it put her in a good mood the entire day. A zing passed through her chest, and she felt the tears pool in her eyes. The day was still young, and already she was incredibly moved. Today, the weather in her heart would surely be a bright and cloudless day.

As the song ended, Jieun got up and stretched. She changed out of her pyjamas, stuffed them into the washing machine, added the detergent, and pressed the start button. Towels, underwear and pyjamas spun in the drum, white bubbles forming as they hugged and rubbed the grime off one another. Just as a candle burns itself to make light, the tumbling clothes were washing each other clean. *There's light all around us. We may not see it, but it's always there.* Jieun sat in front of the washing machine, mulling over her thoughts.

Is it really the same – washing off stains on hearts and washing dirty laundry? Or are they different? Can I really use my abilities to the fullest? Will that break the spell – allow me to grow old and die? She'd been the one to bind herself to the promise, but she had no idea how to break free of it. *If only Mum were by my side.* Her heart gave a squeeze.

'Why is it hurting so much these days?'

Placing a palm against her chest, she took several deep breaths, closed her eyes and imagined the pain erased. She couldn't afford to fall sick today. She had a premonition – an important guest was coming. Gradually, the pain subsided. Was it because of her earnest pleas, or would it have eased up anyway? She wasn't sure.

Thoughts and feelings tumbled inside her; it was time to do some cleaning. Whenever the going got tough, or she was at a loss to know what to do, or when frustration threatened to overwhelm her, she would fall back on her long-time habit of cleaning. Fold the bedding, throw away the unnecessary, and return each item to its original position. Open the windows, dust the surfaces, wash the plates clean and wipe the mirror. As she cleaned and decluttered, the dust in her heart also seemed to be obliterated. Mirrors were always left to the last. So that when they were sparkling, she could see herself more clearly.

A cool breeze drifted in from the opened windows, clearing the stuffiness in the room. She took out a roll of kimbap from the refrigerator, and while it heated up in the microwave she boiled some water to make tea.

She remembered how her mother had smelled of delicious tea. 'Drinking tea is about comforting the heart,' she used to tell little Jieun. 'From brewing the tea to sipping it, the whole routine soothes our feelings.' Back in Jieun's kitchen, the crisp wind blew, signalling the onset of winter. *Time for some warm tea and breakfast before heading to the laundry.*

The microwave beeped. She took out the kimbap, and somewhere within her, her mother's warm voice seemed to ring out.

'Do you know the magic spell for a lovely day?' her mother had asked as she sipped her tea. 'In the morning, tell yourself to look forward to something amazing, and it'll come true. So, my dear child, keep smiling and have a fantastic day. I love you.'

I miss you. There's a saying that ardent longing can turn into a star shining brightly in the sky. She looked out, imagining the sky at night. It was as if she were looking into her mother's eyes. Jieun took a deep breath. *That's right, I'll look forward to today. Something amazing will happen. I'm sure.*

Chapter X

THE CHILD

'Sajangnim, delivery for you!' Uncle Yeonghui called out to Jieun.

Ever since his visit to the mind laundry, he'd begun spending more time talking to people, his gaze no longer averted. In the past, he used to dip his head in greeting and turn away right after handing over the parcels, but these days he often stayed on for a chat.

His notebook, which used to be an obsessive record of time, was now filled with poems. He even started a blog – *Morning Greetings from a Deliveryman* – and interacted with his readers. Yeonghui no longer had his back turned against the world. Nor was the door to his heart firmly shut. One step at a time, he was learning how to open up.

After erasing his penchant for wallowing in self-blame, Yeonghui felt as though he'd been reborn. *Things happen. It wasn't me. It wasn't my fault.* He decided to stop dwelling on his past and learn to look forward. The painful memories remained, but he no longer trapped himself in thinking that he was to blame, or that if he'd done better, none of it would have happened.

His heart found peace, and for the first time in his life he was happy. Nothing had really changed, yet he felt like he was living in a brand-new today. All it had taken was a change of mindset.

'I heard your story on the radio,' Jieun said, taking the package and passing him a glass of water.

Yeonghui scratched his head awkwardly, but there was a hint of a smile on his face as he nodded in thanks and gulped down the iced water.

'It's embarrassing. I didn't think they'd pick mine.' He chuckled.

It was the first time she was seeing his teeth in a wide smile, and it mirrored on her face. Like good vibes, smiles are infectious. The air, too, felt gentle and calm.

'Sajangnim, do you know what's the most amazing thing I've learned from writing poetry?'

Jieun bit her lip, mulling over his question.

'Um . . . that you can express emotions through words?'

'That's a good point. But what really hits me is how you can always rewrite if you make a mistake. It's easy, especially when I use a pencil. I can just erase it or cross it out. It'll leave some marks, for sure, but they're proof that I've given thought to something, and I like that feeling.'

'Indeed. It's the same in life. If we make a mistake, we can also rub away some bits and try again.'

'Yes. It never occurred to me that I was allowed a second

chance. I was fixated on the idea that if I got it wrong, it'd stay that way. All my life, I believed that there can only be one right answer. But in fact it's OK to scribble something messy, and I'm always free to rewrite and try again.'

'I'm happy that you figured that out. I've been around for a much longer time than you'd imagine, but this is a nugget of wisdom that I've only come to realize recently. You're doing much better than me.'

Their conversation flowed with the ease and camaraderie of long-time friends. Just then, a pair of eyes peeked out from behind Yeonghui.

'Oh! Hey, there. Who might you be?' Jieun asked.

The child looked to be about ten years old. She stared at Jieun, and silently retreated behind Yeonghui again.

'Couple of days back, this kid started following me. She'd tag along for a few hours as I went about my work, and then trot away on her own. But I'm moving bulky items today and I don't want her to get hurt. Can you take her for a while?'

'Sure.'

'She'll leave when she needs to, so don't worry. Oh . . . There's something else I wanted to tell you. Since that day, I have a much easier time falling asleep and I feel much more refreshed every morning. It's all thanks to you.'

'I'm glad to hear that.'

The child had poked her head out again and was staring curiously at her surroundings. She was wearing a yellow dress, her hair nicely braided in plaits and her cheeks were round like dumplings. Jieun bent down, picked a flower from a vine and held it out to her.

'Hello. I'm Jieun. Do you want to see something fun?'

Nodding, the child hopped out from behind Yeonghui, who dipped his head and left. Jieun cupped the flower in her hands and flicked her wrists – twice. The child moved forward, her lips puckering in curiosity.

'Blow twice here,' Jieun said.

Huu huu. The little girl puffed. Jieun spread out her fingers, and from her palms petals fluttered out like butterflies. The child gasped.

The petals flew higher and higher, and the young girl ran after them, hands outstretched to catch their tails. For a while they played, and when she came back Jieun held out her palms and opened them again. This time, they held a cookie. The little girl stuffed the treat into her mouth, munching as she ran towards the front garden. Like a bird, she spread out her arms and flapped, chasing after the petals. After a while, she ran back to Jieun, who squatted down to meet the child at eye level. In those bright, clear eyes, Jieun saw her reflection and when the child's lashes fluttered, it was as if Jieun was also blinking in her eyes.

'Where do you live?'

'I don't have a house.'

'You don't? Then where do you sleep?' Jieun pretended to be astonished.

The child looked left and right, as if not wanting to be overheard before she cupped her hands around her mouth and stepped closer.

'Tell you a secret,' she whispered into Jieun's ear. 'I'm a princess from the moon. Everywhere is home.'

'That's so lovely. Then how about your mummy and daddy?'

'I don't have a mummy or daddy.'

There was a pause.

Taken aback by her matter-of-fact tone, Jieun held the child's hand in silence. The young girl continued to chew her cookie as her lashes fluttered over her shining eyes.

'Well, I don't have a daddy or mummy either,' said Jieun.

'Really? Then we're the same.'

'What's your name?'

'I don't have one.'

Glancing at the child, a memory flashed through Jieun's mind – the day she'd stepped into Our Snack Shop for the first time. Had she ended up here because she was craving the warmth of humans? Back then, like the child, she'd had neither a name nor parents. But now she was living as Jieun, who knew how to smile and be with others.

'I didn't have one, either. Looks like we are pretty similar.'

'You, too? All right, then, I'll tell you one more secret. I'm going to build a world full of peace, where nobody hates each other. That's why I'm here.'

Her words rang out loud and clear. *A princess? Build a world without hate?* Looking into her bright eyes, Jieun thought back to the village she'd left behind so long ago. Indeed, such a world had existed. In her hometown nobody knew what hate was, and spring always followed autumn.

'That sounds amazing. My dear princess, how about I give you a name you can use while you're here?'

'Um. All right, then.'

The child spoke as if she were doing Jieun a huge favour,

at which Jieun folded her arms and pretended to be deep in thought.

'Since you're making a new world, how about spring – the time when new life sprouts? From now on, you'll be *Bommie*.'

'Bommie?'

'Yes, the season when beautiful flowers, like yourself, bloom. A long, long time ago, I used to live in a village where spring followed autumn, and after spring autumn returned once more. Like the world you want to make, there weren't any bad feelings at all. I'd love to live in such a place again. Will you make it happen?'

'*Bommie* . . . I like it. And I'll do it!'

Bommie flashed a huge grin brighter than the sun. Buoyed up, the petals resting in the corner twitched and swirled up again.

With a spring in her step, Bommie bounced up the staircase leading to the rooftop. Jieun followed behind.

On the rooftop, Bommie made a beeline for the laundry lines, weaving merrily in and out among the t-shirts with open arms. The sky was a clear blue, not a single cloud could be seen. A light breeze blew, tickling their foreheads and frisking the laundry dry. Among the fluttering t-shirts, Bommie played tag with the petals, her bubbly laughter spreading far and wide.

Jieun, too, smiled as she looked up at the sky. Her fingers laced through her hair, smoothing the billowing strands dancing in the wind. She took a deep breath, closed her eyes, and spread out her arms to feel the rush of the breeze. The suffocating sensation gripping her heart seemed to retreat. *I'm no longer sad*. Here in Marigold, the happiness that she'd thought she'd never experience seemed to be within reach.

'I'll draw you a picture as a gift!'

Bommie's voice appeared from behind as she hugged Jieun around the waist. When Jieun turned around, Bommie held her grip and looked up. *What an honest and trusting child*. Her energy seemed to spread to Jieun as well. At the flick of her wrist, one of the petals turned into a box of marker pens. Bommie bounced happily towards the laundry lines and returned with a white shirt.

'Can I draw it on here?'

'Sure, go ahead. I can't wait to see it.'

Bommie spread the t-shirt on the ground and doodled enthusiastically. Jieun looked on, her thoughts adrift. *What does happiness mean?*

Outside the window, the weather is beyond our control. The sun will rise and set every day, sometimes there'll be rain, and at night the moon and stars light up the sky blanketed by the darkness, and when the night gives way to dawn, it'll be yet another day. There's nothing we can do to change what's outside, but we can choose the weather in our heart. Our feelings are ours to decide, and there's always happiness within us. The weather in our heart is ours, and ours alone.

By choosing to be happy, even when the days are full of thunderstorms, the gentle moonlight in our hearts can still bring about peace. By choosing to love, our hearts are filled. Life may be full of sadness, but if we choose to smile, we'll find joy even if it's a tough world out there. And to have an easier life, perhaps the secret is . . .

'I'm done! This is your gift – a world with only peace and no hate!'

Stirring out of her reverie, Jieun accepted the t-shirt. Bommie stood, eagerly awaiting Jieun's reaction. When Jieun unfolded the shirt, her mind went blank. For a long minute, she stared at the drawing before sweeping Bommie into her arms.

'This is the peaceful world you wanted to make? It's beautiful.'

Bommie squirmed out of Jieun's embrace to run after the petals. Jieun's gaze returned to the t-shirt.

Using the colourful markers, Bommie had drawn a two-storey house and among the flowers and butterflies were the letters in childish handwriting: The Mind Laundry.

Jieun had been searching for her hometown for so long, and here it was, right in front of her. That moment, the unfinished sentence flashed through her mind.

The secret is in this very moment.

The light of happiness shines bright – not in the sky that's out of reach, but in the glow in our hearts. It's always in us. Right now, in this moment. The past cannot be undone; the future is still far ahead, so what we should focus on is *today* – the time we're living in. Step sideways and the moment has passed, but taking a step forward brings us not to the future, but to the present.

When we stew in the regrets of yesterday, or obsess about tomorrow, we lose sight of today. Because she'd chosen to carry the heavy burden of sadness and remorse, no matter how many times she was reborn Jieun had never once enjoyed the happiness of the moment. On occasions when it was within reach, she'd flee as though she didn't deserve to be anywhere near bliss. But was that what her parents would have wanted for her? To be shackled to the past, to be afraid of happiness?

Jieun slumped to the floor, hugging the t-shirt close to her. The petals hovered over her anxiously. It was as if Jieun had turned to stone. Her eyes were unfocused, staring vacantly at the sky. Without warning, her vision blurred and hot tears rolled down her cheeks. They fell silently, glowing blue as they splashed and streaked patterns on her dress. The petals flapped their wings. In the eye of the whirlpool was Bommie, whose gaze was fixed on Jieun. With a rustle, Bommie slowly disintegrated into red petals, swooping into Jieun's black dress. In that moment, Jieun thought she knew who Bommie was. She reached out, desperately grasping at the petals. Yellow dress; red, rosy cheeks.

That child was her.

Happy days playing with her mother in their garden; those blissful memories were by her side all the while, woven into the petals. What about all her other precious memories? Were they here, too? All the time she was wallowing in loneliness, was she never once alone? As the memories came rushing back the floodgates opened, and she burst out crying. She buried her head in the dress – now streaked with blue and red petals – and her frail shoulders trembled as she howled. In that moment the wind died down, and the laundry fell limp. And those who cared for her paused in their tracks.

★

Downstairs, the ajumma and Yeonhee, who'd ended work early, exchanged glances. Yeonhee's eyes were deep with worry.

'. . . Is she all right? Should we go up? Seems like something's happened . . .'

'Don't worry. It'll pass, like everything else. Sounds impossible, doesn't it? But it's true. Whether it's good or bad, nothing will stay the same. When you feel like crying, do it. And if you're happy, laugh to your heart's content. And this too shall pass. When you've come to the end of the end and looked fear in the eye, you'll be ready to start afresh.'

'. . . All right,' said Yeonhee. 'But Jieun sajangnim always looks so sad.'

'Indeed. But remember, all of us were born to seek happiness, so she, too, is on her way to find hers. Let's keep faith. Come on, we should go,' said the ajumma as she patted Yeonhee's shoulders. 'If she knows we're here, it's going to make her worry . . .'

The ajumma shuffled back to her shop. Time to prepare a fresh batch of rice for the kimbap, cooked with a generous amount of warmth and love. A warm, well-fed stomach would help the sadness to pass.

Meanwhile, Yeonhee flipped the laundry's sign to CLOSED.

At times, darkness appeared clearer than glass, brighter than light. Above Jieun, who was now racked with sobs, the moon hid its face, and the stars dimmed their light. Tonight, not a single cloud hung in the sky.

Sometimes darkness stretches longer than the day. But all it takes to soothe sorrow is a thoughtful gesture. The night is deep to allow us the freedom to grieve and be sad, but when dawn breaks, it is telling us to stop crying and move forward. Nobody knows what the rising sun will bring, but at the very least, in its ascent, it quietly splits the night in two. True, the night is deep, but the care people feel for one another runs even deeper.

Chapter XI

JIEUN

Who am I? Where did I come from, and where am I going?

If only her wretched life could end. She could not let go of this thought, musing on it often, perhaps too often. Why did she have to suffer so much? She desperately yearned to turn back time, to set things right again. The agony of losing her parents swallowed her whole, but she submitted herself to the pain, accepting it as the punishment she deserved for her split-second mistake.

Whenever she got the slightest taste of a happy, ordinary life, she'd flee to her next life. *I don't deserve happiness yet*, she reminded herself. She had to find her family first, even if it meant that she must continue to wander through time and space. Only then would she be able to end her misery, and be happy again – with her parents by her side. That single thought had sustained her through each day in the never-ending stretch of time. It never occurred to her that she was lonely because bitterness had long become part of her. She was used to it. Or rather, she believed she was used to it.

How was it possible that, even after all this time, she still couldn't find her parents? Life felt like one big joke, throwing questions at her when there were never any answers in the first place. And now that she wanted to give up, to release herself from her powers and seek death, she was smiling a lot more, spending time with others over meals and conversations, and enjoying the breath of the wind and the scents it carried.

It made her greedy for more. How cunning of life. Despite knowing that nothing would last forever, she found herself wishing for eternity. Like the saying goes, life's a sweet dream that you won't want to wake up from. She wished she'd never have to wake up from the sweet dream here in Marigold.

But what was the life she truly wanted? Had she even thought about that? Day after day, she lived as though she'd forgotten what life was. Or perhaps she pretended not to remember. All those questions she had no answers to washed over her, night after night.

Her heart gave a squeeze. She lifted her right hand and gently placed it over her chest, her other hand on top, as if cradling her heart. A wave of energy rippled within her, and red petals started streaming out in a ribbon, wrapping her in their embrace. *They are outside the circle, and I'm inside.* She closed her eyes, letting the voices flow like music in her.

'If only I could take out my mind, wash it thoroughly, and stick it back in.'

'If only. Wouldn't we be happier without all these painful memories?'

'Help me get rid of the stain left by love.'

'When life is so dazzling, it's lonely.'

'Aren't you curious about the petals appearing from the clothes?'

'I was praying for the peace and wellbeing of others. As though I'm lighting candles in my heart.'

'Just help me smooth out the creases and make the memories less painful to recall.'

'I want to reset my life and start afresh.'

Where do my words end, and where do yours begin?

'It's lovely to have the power to empathize and heal, but if she knows of her ability to make wishes come true . . . won't she become afraid to dream or to make wishes?'

A voice spoke. Jieun tried to focus on the memory, but all she could make out was a blurry silhouette. How was it possible that she'd pulled through such a long stretch of time on a single longing, yet she could no longer remember the faces of those she missed the most? Her heart ached as though it had been pierced. She slumped to the ground, her breathing harsh and ragged. Without warning, the petals accelerated in the opposite direction and became a blur of orange. What was happening?

She lowered her hands. In a split second, the orange petals rushed into her heart. She grasped at the last petal and turned it on her palm. It was a marigold flower. Cradling it, she whispered its meaning.

'*The happiness that'll come* . . . But what is happiness . . . ? How do I become happy? I don't know. But I want to stop regretting, to stop wandering aimlessly. I want to live in this moment, today. If only . . .'

It was then. The marigold petals whooshed out in a heartbeat, turning back into the red camellia before becoming a flutter of blue. Forget-me-nots. Mirroring the brilliant colour of the sea, they spread like light as they flew up to the sky, scattering downwards as blue rain. The petals became puddles, a lake and the sea, only stopping when the sea of blue stretched out to the horizon, undulating calmly. The sky and the sea became one and the same. Slowly, she fell into its embrace.

Splash!

She'd forgotten how to swim. She wasn't pretending – she'd really forgotten. Spreading her arms wide, she relaxed and slowly gave herself to the sea. A sense of calm enveloped her, as if she were back in her mother's arms. *Where is it taking me?* She sank deeper, and her thoughts drifted to the language of the blue flowers covering her.

Don't forget me.

No, it's OK to forget me. Forget me, please.

The water was calm. As if nothing had happened.

I became the bubbles, the sea, the sky.

. . . I became blue light. I became petals.

And now, I am free.

Chapter XII

MOTHER

Ddi di di di, ddi di di di, ddi di di di—

At the alarm, her eyes snapped open. Her head was throbbing, and her body burned. She ran a hand through her hair, sweeping it back before closing her eyes again. With no energy to prop herself up, she remained lying down and rested an arm on her forehead. Her body ached as though she'd just squeezed out through a wormhole.

'Was it a dream? But it felt so real.'

Jieun remembered the embrace of the sea. The petals had moved like fins, propelling her forward, and for the first time in a long while she had laughed. She paddled along in the waters and closed her eyes, but when she next opened them she was back in her bed.

'Swimming with fins? Ha. Am I a mermaid, or what! How cheesy.'

Coughing, she tried to sit up again. Her clothes and hair were wet – from sweat or water, she couldn't tell. Could it really have happened? She pulled open a drawer in her bedside table and took out a thermometer. She inserted the tip into her right ear and pressed the button.

'Thirty-eight . . . I wonder if I still have fever medicine.'

She was about to check her first-aid box for something to ease the fever and headache when a wave of dizziness hit her. She took a deep breath, steadying herself before standing up again. In the kitchen she popped the pills, swallowing them with a gulp of water before searching for her phone. She was scrolling through missed calls and messages from Jaeha, Yeon-hee and the ajumma when she suddenly paused. *Hmm.* She had fallen asleep . . . on Wednesday night. But today was already Friday. She'd been knocked out for two whole days. What had happened? Was it *not* a dream?

–Don't worry. I'm fine.–

She remembered meeting Bommie, and it seemed like afterwards she'd plunged into a meandering, feverish dream of being submerged in the sea. Over the years, consumed by sadness, regret and self-blame, she had long forgotten the happiness that she'd once enjoyed. And when she met Bommie, those happy times crashed upon her, wave after wave. Bommie was her – the happy child she'd once been. She'd had always been there with her, living all along as the petals on her dress. In that case, were Mum and Dad also nearby? Perhaps they were the petals or the villagers or the wind or sunshine or moonlight?

'Maybe they were also crossing worlds in search of me.

Were they those villagers I felt inexplicably drawn towards? Did I simply not recognize them . . . ?'

If her parents were really watching over her, she couldn't continue to wallow in self-blame. *They wouldn't have wanted me to live such a sad and empty life. Maybe it's time to finally stop punishing myself. To waste the time given to me is perhaps the worst thing to do.*

She wiped away her sweat and changed out of her clothes, tossing them into the laundry basket before stepping into the shower. As she pulled the lever the water came cascading down, along with the memories of her dream. Wrapped in a huge towel, she searched for the black dress she wore every day. Red petals scattered across the dress, not the blue forget-me-nots she remembered from yesterday. Was it a dream after all? But her shoulders ached as if she'd been swimming the whole day. She rubbed them vigorously. The medicine must be working, because she could feel the fever subsiding.

'Wouldn't it be nice if we could swallow some salve if our heart is feeling a little bruised? But that isn't quite possible, so Mummy will make you a special cup of sweet, warm cocoa instead. Drink up and go to bed. By the time you wake up tomorrow, half the things that made you upset will have vanished. You might even feel magically happy. Come here, my dear child.'

Whenever Jieun was grumpy, her mother would take a mug larger than her face and make her a huge cup of cocoa topped with marshmallows. Even on the days she bawled or when her lips were pursed into a taut line, once she tasted the sweetness of the cocoa the frustrations would melt away like the marshmallows floating on the top. It was as if the drink contained magic.

Even though her mother didn't possess the wondrous powers of the villagers, in Jieun's eyes she was like a magician who never failed to soothe her feelings. Her apron always smelled of delicious cookies and her scarf gave off a lovely floral scent. Jieun loved to bury her face in her apron and breathe in the aromas, or to hug her tight and smell the flowers. Jieun grew up with love, her cheeks round and rosy from the delectable treats being whipped up in her mother's kitchen all the time.

Her mother was smiley and warm, but even so, there were moments Jieun had caught her staring off into the distance and sighing. When autumn rounded the corner, she would look out of the window with an expression of longing, and for a while she'd be unusually still before going to the kitchen. In a huge pot, she'd pour in a generous serving of wine, along with oranges, apples, pears, cinnamon sticks, drizzling in five rounds of her best honey before putting it all to a boil. The fruits were washed clean before going into the pot, and they were always the prettiest and tastiest-looking ones she could buy. Whenever her mother made it, the house would be enveloped in a vapour of ripe grapes.

'Mummy, can I have some?' Jieun would ask, lingering by the kitchen. Despite her warm smile, her mother was firm as she shook her head.

'This is a special concoction for Mummy; I can't share it with anyone else. When you grow up, I'll pass the recipe to you and you can make your own brew.'

Her mother's eyes crinkled teasingly and the vitality that had been sapped from her seemed to return. And after she drank the tea, she was back to her usual self. Before that, her eyes were full of sadness, as if there were something or someone she dearly missed.

Back then, her mother had probably been the same age as Jieun looked now. Jieun and her dad used to call it *the season of longing* when her mother started to make her concoction again. Was she missing what she'd left behind in the days before meeting Dad? Why didn't she seek it out again? Was she planning to let her yearning remain in her heart? Was that what it meant to be a grown-up?

Little Jieun had raised a hand to pat her mother on her shoulder, and she responded by grasping Jieun's hand and pulling her into a hug. Jieun loved how their warmth would meld comfortingly in the embrace. There was something melancholic yet beautiful about it.

'Should I make something for myself today? A special brew like Mum's?'

At home, the tea she drank was made with store-bought tea leaves. Only the tea she served to her visitors was brewed with care, from ingredients she'd painstakingly dried in the wind. Because of the sincerity and heart that went into that tea, it felt much warmer than what she drank at home in the mornings. Despite brewing healing tea for others, she'd never once made it specifically for herself.

Even if she hadn't managed to inherit her mother's recipe, Jieun thought she should be able to make it on her own. As she set the kettle to boil, she took out her favourite white teacup.

'Today's special ingredient is . . . my heartfelt wish to be happy.'

The secret to the healing tea was her own sincerity steeped in the brew.

Today, she would include a generous serving for herself. While the water was boiling, the petals began to rustle at her feet. Closing her eyes, she lifted her hands like a conductor, and at the wave of her hand, the petals glided into the kettle. Instead of dried tea leaves, today she would use fresh petals.

If Mum and Dad had been by her side, they would have been terribly upset to see that she had lived a withered life full of regrets. If they'd seen how she lost her rounded cheeks and shrivelled into a bony, pale frame, and how she'd withdrawn herself from the world, even if they were to be reunited they'd be so much sadder than she was. Jieun pondered how healthy she used to look – her rosy cheeks, the colour in her face. Her thoughts drifted back to her mother's kitchen, full of laughter and love, and the garden she'd played in with her dad.

She opened her eyes and poured the special brew into the teacup, which as usual she'd warmed beforehand. The red liquid streamed out steadily, filling the cup. Not too much, not too little – just the right amount.

While the tea was cooling, she went into the living room and opened the windows. As on her first day in the apartment, she walked out on to the veranda, closed her eyes, and took a deep breath. The smell of the nearby city mixed with the sea rushed into her senses. Her eyes opened. She held out her arm, her fingers curved around the air, and the teacup came zooming into the arch of her palm without spilling. The sky had turned a brilliant red, tinting the clouds as the sun set.

'Even if the moon is bright tonight, it'll be shrouded by all those clouds.'

She sipped her one-of-a-kind concoction, its warmth spreading and filling her with happiness. Nothing had changed from yesterday, yet today felt different. *The happiness that'll come*. She was reminded of the marigolds. Right now, that happiness was in her tea.

As she swallowed the last drop, the petals on her dress peeled away and swirled up in a wind. They'd been a part of her for so long, but now they were all heading into the fiery sunset. Jieun waved her hand. The clouds descended to surround her, the softness of their touch like her mother's embrace. Jieun relaxed. *One, two, three* . . . The clouds slid back up into the sky. Jieun turned to walk back into the house, stopping in front of the mirror by the entrance.

The clouds had left a trail in their wake. Her black dress was transformed into a fluffy white. Where the red patterns had been, blue petals took their place. A hint of red spread across her lips, lighting up her pale face. Strange. It felt like hope was welling inside her.

She was seized with a sudden desire to be at the laundry. *Wouldn't it be lovely if I could open this door and walk straight in?*

'Oh gosh. What just happened?'

Jieun stepped right in, a look of surprise on her face at how her wish had come true on her first attempt. For the sake of those who'd been worried about her, the first thing she did was to turn on the lights on the sign before going around the house to open the windows. Then she headed up to the rooftop. The clothes she'd hung out to dry two days ago were still fluttering in the wind.

Even this laundry needed both the sun and the wind for drying. Mightn't our hearts be the same – needing both warmth and cold, happiness as well as sadness?

She'd spent the bulk of her life escaping. Now, it was time for her to anchor herself. Like the laundry, perhaps she could let herself flow with the motions of life – get wet when it rained, ride the wind when it blew and enjoy the warmth when the sun was out. Learn to look at herself swaying to the wind, love herself for who she was – an inadequate person, someone who made mistakes, at times wandering like a lost sheep. Perhaps this was truly the secret to letting go of the stains on our hearts.

'Omo! Jieun sajangnim! What's the occasion? You're in white today! How gorgeous! You should wear it more often!'

'Sajangnim! We were so worried that you'd fallen sick! Why didn't you pick up our calls?'

'I was so stressed about something bad happening to you that I ended up chewing two strands of squid at the same time and almost pulled out my teeth! You owe me one!'

At the sight of the lights, the snack shop ajumma, Yeonhee and Jaeha hurried up to the rooftop. There was an outpouring of concern in their rebukes. Jieun's lips cracked into a wide grin, and she tried to cover her mouth with her hands as they rushed to embrace her.

'I'm . . . hungry. I want to eat something.'

Three pairs of eyes stared at her in surprise. It was the first time they'd heard her saying she wanted to eat. Ajumma quickly returned to her shop to prepare. Jaeha and Yeonhee linked an arm each with Jieun and went downstairs.

'Sajangnim, have the petals turned blue?'

Jaeha's eyes widened as his gaze landed on her dress. He remembered how he'd once seen a flash of blue or purple, and wondered if it was his eyes playing tricks on him again.

'Aren't they just as pretty?' Jieun replied.

The day the laundry came into existence, these two children were also by her side. She remembered how the moon had been shrouded behind the clouds, and the world had seemed to be blanketed by an inky black. It had been a cloudy day, just like today.

'Sajangnim! Can you tell us in advance if you're going to fall sick? Do you know how worried we were? You were already as white as a sheet, and suddenly you went completely off-grid. We were frantic!'

Yeonhee had chided Jieun gently as she unbuttoned her black work jacket. For the two days that she was missing, Jaeha and Yeonhee had stewed in worry. They'd briefly considered making a police report, but, on second thoughts, was Jieun someone that the police could track down?

'We tried knocking on your house door, too. If you still didn't appear, we were planning to go straight to the police! But imagine us having to tell them that we were looking for a pretty woman with long hair who knew magic, and she was last seen in a dress with a floral pattern! They'd think we'd lost our minds and take *us* in instead!'

Jieun was apologetic and thankful at the same time. Was this what it meant to feel a sense of belonging? She placed her palms together and bowed her head.

'Sorry, I was a little unwell.'

Yeonhee hurriedly placed a palm to Jieun's forehead, thinking to herself, *Since when does she ever apologize? Has she hurt her head?*

'Sajangnim, are you very unwell? I hope it's not something serious. Why are you apologizing! Don't scare us . . . And why, today of all days, have you decided to change into this gorgeous white dress? You're so different from your usual self. Are you even Jieun sajangnim? Did you make a clone of yourself?'

'Take your hand away and stop talking nonsense!' Jieun swiped Yeonhee's hand away. The two of them simultaneously ran a hand down their chests in relief.

'OK. Still the sajangnim we know.'

'Aigoo, stop teasing her. Come, eat before the food gets cold.'

The ajumma set down a plate of thickly sliced kimbap in front of each of them.

'Oh my. Is this even kimbap when it's as big as my face? Ajumma, how am I supposed to eat this? We'll need a knife and fork!'

'Jaeha, you rascal. Slice it, cut it, whatever – just eat it! And don't talk so much! I'll bring the soup, give me a second.'

Laughing, the ajumma smacked his back and limped past them to get the soup. Yeonhee quickly stood up to distribute the bowls.

Jieun and Jaeha stared at the gigantic kimbap in front of them. Jaeha was the first one to reach out with his chopsticks – he stretched his jaw and stuffed a piece into his mouth. The fluffy, freshly cooked rice was coated with the fragrance of the sesame oil, and just the right touch of salt. There were no other condiments, and inside the roll were sliced carrots, cucumber, burdock, egg strips, ham, yellow radish and fish cake. Each time he chewed, he could taste a different ingredient. Kimbap reminded him of Ms Yeonja. Because Jaeha was a picky eater, his mother often rolled kimbaps for him to make sure that he had a well-balanced diet. The thought of his mother drew his chest tight, and despite his already bulging cheeks, he stuffed another piece in and drank a mouthful of soup.

'Ajumma, this tastes much better than usual. What did you put in it? Tell me, tell me!'

The tears were threatening to well up, so Jaeha spoke louder and more enthusiastically to hide his emotions. The ajumma tucked her hands in her apron and smiled. She had switched up the ingredients after Yeonja came by the other day. *Don't fry the carrots and cucumbers, or it'll be too salty. Don't julienne it, either.* She'd simply followed Yeonja's advice.

'Eat up if it's good. I can make more for you.'

With their chopsticks, the four of them worked their way through the kimbap. Jieun took a piece and dismantled it, choosing to eat some of the fillings first.

Yeonhee simply stuffed an entire piece into her mouth. With back-to-back training sessions all day, running around in her heels and work suit, she hadn't even had time for lunch. She was glad to finally catch a breather, and the day's tension melted away. For a while, nobody spoke as they chewed their food. A comfortable silence flowed; they didn't need small talk to feel at ease with one another. Having made a dent in his mountain, Jaeha broke the silence.

'Look at us eating together. Don't we seem like a family?'

Jieun, Yeonhee and the ajumma exchanged warm glances. *Hmm, but what really is family*?

Jieun had spent many, many years wandering among the worlds. The warm memories of her childhood had been the only thing that kept her afloat through the lonely, difficult times. But right now, at this moment, she felt at peace, as though she'd returned to the good old days. She was no longer lonely. Even if she never found her parents again, she wasn't going to wallow in sadness. Whatever had happened was behind her; she would look ahead. *Accept and acknowledge the past, live in the present – have I mustered the courage to do so?* She tilted her head, tapping absently at the empty soup bowl with her spoon.

'Aigoo. Family is no big deal, my dears. So many of us wish we could cut off our family members who get into trouble all the time and make life difficult for everyone else – if only we weren't bound by blood! They give us only worry and hate, yet because they're family, we can't help but have expectations, only to get hurt or inflict hurt when they fall short. These days, we look for our chosen family – people on the same wavelength who come together in support of one another, just like us. Don't you think that's more like family?'

Dragging her bad leg, the ajumma brought some fish cake soup over and set it in front of Jieun, winking as she spoke. Her wrinkled face was affectionate, and Jieun broke into a smile as she doled out more soup. *How warm and comforting. The soup, the company.*

'You're right. Family is about supporting one another, eating together, and sharing our lives. We're a family.'

Tears began to pool in Yeonhee's eyes. *Do I have a family now? The shelter I yearned for?*

'Hey. Why's the mood like this? It's supposed to be a happy occasion. Anyway, I need to call Hae-in. He was super-worried when you went off-grid. He kept checking in to see if we'd found you, even though he has his hands full with his photo exhibit. It's opening tomorrow. He should be focusing on that, but for the past two evenings all he's done is to go around the neighbourhood hoping to find you.'

Jaeha rubbed his belly as he held his phone, all the while sneaking glances at Jieun. He thought of an old saying: there are three things in the world that can't be hidden: poverty, love and a sneeze. It hadn't taken him long to cotton on to Hae-in's feelings. When he saw how Hae-in's eyes followed Jieun on his first visit to the laundry, he was honestly a little worried. Jieun was someone who could suddenly disappear with the wind. Just as she'd suddenly appeared in the village, she might one day vanish without a trace.

But it had been a long time since he'd seen Hae-in fretting over someone like this. Hae-in might seem friendly, but deep down he set clear boundaries and wasn't the type to give away his heart easily.

'Oh . . . I see . . .' Jieun murmured as she picked at her dismembered kimbap.

Jaeha couldn't tell what she was thinking. She was standoffish, but friendly; cold but also warm. She was a good person who helped others with the pain in their hearts, yet she seemed to be clueless when it came to dealing with her own pain. She was good at reading the emotions in people's eyes, but her own eyes were devoid of feeling, dark, like the sea.

While Yeonhee massaged her sore calves, Jaeha went to get a cup of water for her before texting Hae-in. He wasn't good at dealing with complicated feelings, but as long as his friends were happy right now, he was good. Hae-in must be worried sick, so addressing that was the priority.

A second after Jaeha tapped the send button, his phone rang. It was Hae-in.

'Jaeha, you found Jieun-ssi? Was she hurt? Is she OK?'

At the barrage of questions, Jaeha simply passed his phone to Jieun. It wasn't his voice Hae-in wanted to hear. Jieun took the phone and stepped outside. She tucked the flyaway strands of hair behind her ear, taking one step towards Hae-in on the other side of the phone.

'I'm all right. I just slept for the past two days. Nothing happened.'

'Jieun-ssi. Did you hurt yourself? Are you very unwell?'

Hearing her voice calmed his anxiety and he breathed a sigh of relief. From the moment he'd first seen her through the viewfinder, the sad look in her eyes had been etched on his heart. It was as if something was lodged in his throat, but when he came to the laundry to see her again, the feeling faded away. It was strange. It wasn't like he'd never fallen in love before, but this yearning to tread carefully and delicately was new to him.

He hoped to be there for this woman who seemed to embody sadness in her entire being even as she sought to heal the hearts of others.

He got the sense that should he make a hasty move, she'd disappear like a drop of water. Hae-in also wanted to be sure of his own feelings. But when Jaeha had told him that Jieun was gone, it had no longer mattered if she was like a water droplet or vapour; if only he could find her again, he was willing to lay bare his feelings. He would do *anything*.

'I . . . Stay there. I'll come to you,' he said as she held the phone to her ear.

At his words, she stepped back again.

'Hello? Jieun-ssi, are you there? I won't be long. Stay there.'

'Um . . . Hae-in-ssi, where are you?'

'I'm at the gallery, but I'll take a cab. I'm only here because I need to prepare for the opening tomorrow.'

'In that case, I'll come to you,' Jieun said. This time, she took two steps forwards.

Hae-in, who was now by the road trying to flag a cab, paused in shock. *She said she's coming. Coming to me.*

'You sure? Aren't you unwell? Don't stretch yourself too thin.'

Hearing the worry in his voice, the corners of her lips turned up in a smile. She had an impulse to try something new, something she'd never done before in Marigold. Because today was a good day with a fair wind.

'Have you heard of the bus with the biggest windows in the world?'

'The bus with the biggest windows in the world? Um . . . I think I know.'

'I'll take that bus and come to you. Then we can talk. Wait for me.'

On each end of the call, they were smiling brightly, a gentle breeze caressing the tops of their heads. As Jieun turned back to the snack shop, her hair danced. Hands hovering over her calves, Yeonhee stared at Jieun in shock.

'Sajangnim . . . is that a bashful smile? What's up with you today? First you said sorry, and now you keep smiling to yourself. I think we need to take you to the hospital!'

'You can go there yourself, Yeonhee. Sajangnim, I'll text you the address.'

Yeonhee was about to say something, but Jaeha stuffed another piece of kimbap into her mouth and chuckled. He wanted to cheer out loud. Just now, he'd pressed his ear against the door, and when he heard Jieun saying that she would go over to Hae-in, he saw how her eyes had begun to shine. She always had a vacant look about her, like a walking corpse. Or else her eyes were full of sadness. This was the first time he saw life in her eyes.

She never left the neighbourhood, yet she'd just told Hae-in she'd go to him at the gallery. Even then, she could always use her magic, but Jaeha clearly heard her say she wanted to ride a bus. What was going on?

'Jaeha, Ms Yeonja told me about the neighbourhood bus. I'll be on my way.'

Pushing open the door, Jieun paused and turned around.

'Ajumma, thanks for the food. It was delicious. Did you say that you liked my dress? I'll find you something similar.'

The three of them stared at her. Why was she behaving so

out of character today? Jieun waved as she stepped out. From now on, she would learn not to ignore the voice in her heart and listen to it instead. Following the pace in her heart, she walked to the bus stop – neither too slow nor too fast. Who knew? One day, she might come to regret walking these steps. But even if she was going to experience heartbreak in the future, it was OK. For now she would muster the courage to go where her heart was leading her.

She headed for the bus with the biggest windows in the world. The bus ride would be her first attempt to knock down the barriers and open the door to her heart. Her footsteps were light and delicate, as if dancing a waltz. The blue petals swayed along to the breeze sweeping the street and her heart.

'The wind is rising. We must try to live.'

Jieun spoke aloud. Her clear voice echoed, reverberating in the alley. At the same time, the streetlamps lit up. Even in the dark, there is always a light shining on the path.

Chapter XIII

BUS RIDE TO THE CITY

'Sajangnim! Here, take this! Even if you have magic, you can't ride a bus without it!'

Huffing and puffing, Jaeha ran to the bus stop and stuffed a bus card into Jieun's hand. Just then, the bus arrived, and Jieun boarded it. *What am I supposed to do with this?* she wondered, walking towards the seat by the biggest window.

'Agasshi!' the bus driver yelled. 'What are you doing? You need to tap here and pay!'

The driver rapped impatiently on the card reader and glared at Jieun. She tapped the card, feeling extra pleased with herself as she sat down. *Wow, there are still things I haven't tried!* Her heart gave a little trill.

She slid open the window and let the wind tickle her cheeks as the bus travelled down the winding road into the city. At every stop, people came on as others got off. There were people with a quick, purposeful stride, some who got down and walked into the embrace of loved ones waiting at the bus stop, tired faces who had their earphones in as they scrolled their phones, friends chatting with one another as they strolled down the street. Inside and outside the bus, everyone was living their own lives. She watched how each of them, with their different expressions and moods, blended into the cityscape.

Strangers passed by one another with an air of indifference, yet they were all together in the same space. Until this moment, Jieun had always felt a sense of alienation no matter what kind of life she was leading. But today she felt like she belonged, and like everyone else, she was sharing the same space. The feeling of harmony eased her heart. *When was the last time I was this relaxed?* There was a sharp twinge in her nose.

'The next stop is Beach Gallery. Beach Gallery.'

She was almost there. Having observed what others did when they were reaching their destination, Jieun pressed the bell. In the distance, she spotted Hae-in at the bus stop, looking uncharacteristically nervous. She felt her heart beating against her chest. The thirty seconds at the traffic light seemed to stretch on much longer.

'Jieun-ssi! Are you OK? Were you very unwell?'

Hae-in, who'd been pacing at the bus stop, rushed forward as soon as she arrived, his eyes roaming her face. He couldn't concentrate on anything at all, not when he'd been beside himself thinking that she'd disappeared. His regrets had gnawed at him. He should have boldly confessed his feelings. In his own way, he'd been trying to get closer to her, but it had never occurred to him that she might vanish. *I should have said something . . .* He regretted his hesitation very much. Jieun gazed at him, taking in his bloodshot eyes and the stubble on his chin.

'I slept for two whole days. I had a dream, and then I woke up. I'm OK now.'

Something had changed in her eyes. Jieun didn't look as sad as she used to. Hae-in was glad. She gave him a reassuring look – she was really fine. No words were needed for them to understand each other. Their hearts hummed in a gentle rhythm.

'Hae-in-ssi, pass me your phone.'

'My phone? Oh . . . Here you go.'

'All right, this is my number. Save it.'

Jieun sent herself a missed call before returning it to him. Carefully, he typed in her name and saved the number. Just seconds ago he'd been thinking about confessing to her, but now that she was in front of him, his mind was blank. *What should I do?* He hesitated.

'Shall we take a walk?'

Jieun answered with a smile. They fell into step.

Against the backdrop of the autumn colours in full display they walked down the footpath, feeling the wind as it swept the smell of the sea towards them. On the road, the traffic ebbed and flowed.

'This is the first time I've been here in the city. It feels like a completely new world, if you know what I mean.'

After a beat, Hae-in replied. 'Yeah, it's different here. It's crowded, people are always in a rush, and our hearts are beating faster, too. So, how does it feel to ride the bus with the biggest windows in the world?'

Was his heart thumping because of the city rush, as he told her, or because she was right next to him? He didn't quite know.

Looking at Hae-in scratch his head, Jieun smiled. *Oh no. Is my heart going haywire? Why is it beating so hard?*

'It was just a bus ride, yet it felt as though my heart had crossed a mountain, stepping into a new world outside the windows. Doesn't life feel like a hiking journey at times? We tell ourselves: once we get over this, things will be better. Yet, once we've crossed one mountain, we come to the next one in no time. But as I got off the bus, it felt as though I didn't have to climb any more, and my heart lightened at the thought. Strange, isn't it?'

Hae-in nodded as though he felt the same way.

'It's probably how people feel when they come to the laundry. I think I understand them better now.'

When Jieun wiped away or soothed the pain of her visitors, she hoped that their hearts would feel more at ease. She felt comforted watching them leave her laundry with a much brighter expression, yet part of her was curious. What was it like? As she lit a candle in her heart and prayed for their happiness, she secretly wished that one day she'd come to experience this feeling herself, but it continued to evade her.

Right now, she dimly felt like she understood. Hae-in kept quiet, not wanting to disturb Jieun and her thoughts. When they reached the gallery, he paused.

'Would you like to take the bus back with me? On our way back to the laundry we can keep each other company.'

'Uhm . . . I'd like that. So, is this the exhibition gallery?'

'Yes. It's the first time I've showcased the photos taken on my mother's camera. Do you want to come in for a bit?'

'Yeah.'

Hae-in had always kept himself closed off from the world. After his parents passed away, he continued to take photos with his mother's camera, but never once did he have the desire to develop the film. What made him feel the first stirrings to unpack his memories was when he'd captured that photo by chance – the teardrop of a woman on the rooftop. He used to believe that a photo could only show the scene for what it was, never the emotions within. But when he caught Jieun's sadness in his frame, he wanted to see it in print.

With the photos developed from his box of film rolls, he decided to rent a ten-pyeong exhibition space in a small gallery, harbouring the hope that she would come and see that photo. Switching on the lights in the gallery, Hae-in gestured for Jieun to enter.

'There's one particular photo I'd like to show you.'

'Oh,' she gasped. 'How did you manage to do this? I didn't think I'd show up in a photo . . .'

At the entrance, Jieun paused, struck by the large photo on display. At the edge of a woman's long black lashes, a teardrop hung against the backdrop of the setting sun.

'Perhaps to other people this is an empty frame. Only you and I can see the photo.'

'How . . . ? Hae-in, are you . . . also . . . ?'

'Oh . . . Uhm . . . That . . . We'll have time to talk about it later. Would you come here for a second?'

Looking at her astonished expression, Hae-in smiled calmly

and gestured to his right. In front of the white wall, set on top of a plastic display cube, was the camera that Hae-in always carried. Next to it was a photo printer, displayed with the sign: *The Decisive Moment.* It was an interactive exhibit where visitors could have their photo taken on the spot.

Hae-in placed his hands on her shoulders and guided Jieun, still looking a little bewildered, to a chair in front of the wall. As she sat down, her gaze lingered on the sign.

'*All my life, I've tried to capture the decisive moments of life, when in fact every moment of life was the decisive moment.* A quote from Henri Cartier-Bresson, right?'

'Yes, that's where I got my inspiration from. Today is such a great day. When I came up with the idea, you were the first person I hoped to take a photo of. Thank you for making that come true.'

Hae-in picked up the camera, smiling shyly as he adjusted the focus. At the same time, a smile mirroring Hae-in's spread across Jieun's face.

'Can I take a photo of you?'

'Sure.'

'Please close your eyes and think back to the happiest moment in your life.'

Jieun closed her eyes. *When was I the happiest?* All this time, she'd thought it would take a very special occasion for her to be that happy again – one she could only experience once she'd atoned for her mistake and put everything right again. Until then, she didn't deserve to be happy.

Yet, she was learning that every moment in life was precious and full of love. Whether it was yesterday, filled with regret;

today, learning how to love herself; or tomorrow, where time might start ticking for her again. No, even if she could never break free and was destined to be stuck in the cycle of rebirths, every single moment of her life was of her own choosing and, hence, she should be happy. She choked up at that thought. She pressed a palm against her chest, feeling the warmth spread.

There were days when she wished she couldn't feel. Then she wouldn't be in pain, nor would she be sad. If only she could wipe away the dust in her heart before putting it back into her chest, if only she could get rid of the pain and sadness. Because it wasn't possible to remove her own heart, was this why she was born with the special power to comfort and heal the pain in others?

Or perhaps she could put emotions on pause when it seemed like the day was going to be a sad one, and to start feeling again only on happy days. But then, would she still be able to feel the pain of others? Would she then be able to pray for their peace as she sent the petals of pain and hurt off into the sunset?

'Ah . . . the petals . . .'

The petals. All along, she'd thought she was alone, but the petals were the manifestations of the feelings of those who'd been by her side. To make sure that she wasn't lonely, the stains of her visitors' sadness had dried to become beautiful crisp petals watching over her. She'd thought she was the one healing others, but in fact they were also comforting her and becoming part of her life, too.

It was only when she accidentally overheard her parents' conversation that she realized she had two powers. Didn't they also mention that the ability to grant wishes was supposed to support the power to comfort and heal?

Love myself, accept myself for who I am, feel the pain, sadness and happiness – isn't today exactly what we've always dreamed of? Perhaps this moment was the secret that Mum and Dad had wanted to tell her. She opened her eyes.

Click.

The photo printer connected to the camera started whirring. Life is always full of surprises. In the photo, her eyes were filled with the laughter of those who'd crossed paths with her – people by her side now, those she'd known over her lifetimes, and her beloved family, whom she missed so dearly.

At that moment, all the petals peeled away from her dress, enveloping Hae-in and Jieun in a whirlwind, spreading boundlessly as they filled the entire gallery.

We don't need magic to make our wishes come true. It's an ability innate in all of us. It comes from the courage and the privilege given by those who love us even as we make mistakes and get hurt in the process. It's not magic given exclusively to the chosen ones, but something both you and I have.

Was this what she had come to the world for? To teach everyone this?

Jieun stared at the photo and at Hae-in in turn. He felt to her like the sun, and like the clothes fluttering on the rooftop. He spread his arms out, his smile as warm as sunshine. Jieun could smell the scent of freshly dried laundry.

'Welcome to the Mind Photo Studio,' said Hae-in.

They burst out laughing. Today was such a beautiful day, shining and gleaming.

A SECRET

'That's just how life is. When there's a difficult situation ahead of us, we wonder – how can we possibly get through this? Yet in times of peace, we're somewhat anxious. What's wrong? Why isn't anything happening? We're always doubting life. If you're feeling that way, come to the mind laundry. Come chat with us. Just by sharing your thoughts, it'll feel as though a stain is being rubbed away from your heart and you'll walk away feeling lighter.'

'Cut! OK. Wow, Lee Yeonhee, you're pretty good at this, huh?'

Jaeha and Yeonhee, who'd been coming over every weekend to help out, had recently started a YouTube channel. Yeonhee was the one who'd suggested it, and volunteered to be in front of the camera since she was used to public-speaking for her job. Jaeha agreed readily; somehow making videos made his heart flutter. On weekdays, he worked hard at his day job, and at the weekend he'd spend the time making videos with Yeonhee.

For Jaeha, life had always felt like sitting on a stationary seesaw. He always seemed to be stuck on the lower end, never bouncing up, but these days he could feel it rising. From the day he'd witnessed the incredible sight of the laundry blooming and mustered the courage to walk in, his seesaw had started to move. It was the bravest he'd been in all his life.

'Why don't you two take over this place?' Jieun commented as she came back with kimbap from the snack shop.

'Sajangnim! We still can't get used to how serious your expression is when you're joking.'

Jaeha pretended to shake in fear as he accepted a roll of kimbap. Yeonhee suddenly stopped. Wait, what was that?

'Sajangnim . . . ! You have white hair? *You?!*'

Shocked, Jieun raised a hand to her head. *White hair?* That was impossible.

'I do? Where?'

'On the right, here . . . Wow. Huge news.'

Jaeha shuffled closer to look for more strands. Now that he was peering so closely, it seemed like Jieun was beginning to develop crow's feet around her eyes. For someone who never seemed to age at all, what was with the sudden white hair and wrinkles?

'Should I pull it out for you?'

'No, leave it. Let me look in the mirror.'

Her steps were light as she went to find a mirror. Was she finally getting her wish – to grow old? To have white hair, to grow fine wrinkles, to stay by the side of those she loved, and to age with them. Was ordinary life finally beginning for her?

Running the mind laundry had made Jieun realize one thing – today is the most special gift. No matter how many regrets you have, yesterday has passed, and tomorrow is the future that has yet to come, so what we should do is to be in the moment, to live our life today. Perhaps the present is the magic given to us.

'Yeonhee, Jaeha, should I tell you a secret?'

'Wow. What kind of secret?'

'Wait, let's check if anyone is listening in.'

'It's OK. We can spread it far and wide.'

'Huh? Then it isn't a secret any more. No fun.'

'No, no! Tell us!'

'Both of you also have a special ability.'

'For real . . . ?'

'It's called *the ability to make whatever you wish come true.*'

Yeonhee and Jaeha stared at each other. Jieun swiped her hair up, and placed a hand on their shoulders.

'I'm on the right path, I made the right choice and things will turn out well. If you believe in it, it'll come true. Within you is the ability to live according to what you say, what you believe in, and where your heart takes you. Don't doubt yourself, have faith. Believe that you can do anything.'

She tapped them twice on their shoulders.

'And remember. The best gifts are wrapped in trials and

tribulations. If you had a tough time today, it means that a gift is soon on its way to you. Maybe you're unwrapping a wonderful surprise.'

She left the two of them to mull over her words and went up to the rooftop. In the middle was a reclining chair. She lay down on it and gazed at the sun. It was too early to send the petals to the sky.

As she basked in the sunlight, she closed her eyes, a peaceful smile spreading across her face, her expression the most relaxed it had ever been. It was hot, but in some sense it wasn't. *At long last, I've figured out my purpose in this world.*

It was a beautiful day to be able, at last, to grow old with the passing of time.

'The perfect weather for a nap.'

ABOUT THE AUTHOR

JUNGEUN YUN is the author of more than ten books, including *Live the Way You Want, Even If I Don't Know How to Be an Adult,* and *To Travel or To Love.* Yun believes that writing is self-reflection, a close examination of emotions; to write is to connect. Yun hosts the podcast *The Path of Books with Jungeun Yun.* She lives in Korea.